MURDER
ON
A WINTER'S
NIGHT

MURDER ON A WINTER'S NIGHT

TEN CLASSIC CRIME STORIES

Edited by Cecily Gayford

Cyril Hare · H. C. Bailey
Margery Allingham · Julian Symons
Dorothy L. Sayers · G. D. H. and M. Cole
Mark Billingham · Arthur Conan Doyle
Ronald Knox · Edmund Crispin

PROFILE BOOKS

First published in Great Britain in 2021 by
PROFILE BOOKS LTD
29 Cloth Fair
London ECIA 7JQ
www.profilebooks.com

Selection copyright © Profile Books, 2021
See p. 199 for individual stories copyright information

1 3 5 7 9 10 8 6 4 2

Typeset in Fournier by MacGuru Ltd
Printed and bound in Great Britain by
CPI Group (UK) Ltd, Croydon CRO 4YY

A CIP catalogue record for this book is available from the British Library.

ISBN 978 1 78816 801 4
eISBN 978 1 78283 852 4

Contents

A Surprise for Christmas

Cyril Hare

They had had their Christmas dinner in the middle of the day because this year there were children in the house. Turkey and plum pudding and all the drinks that rightfully go with them had reduced Jimmy Blenkiron to a pleasant state of somnolence. Lying back in an armchair in front of the library fire, he could just discern the red glow of the logs through his half-shut eyes. His hands still caressed the glass that had held his liqueur brandy. It was half-past three and he was at peace with the world.

Anne Blenkiron came into the room and dropped thankfully on to a sofa beside her husband's chair.

'Thank goodness, there's the washing-up done at last,' she said.

'Good for you,' said Jimmy approvingly. Always a pattern of consideration where his wife was concerned, he shifted his legs slightly to allow some of the warmth from the fire to reach in her direction.

'Why didn't you get the children to help you?' he asked.

'Oh, they're much too busy on their own affairs. They are preparing a surprise for you at tea-time.'

'Wonderful they've got the energy to do anything after what they put away at dinner,' said Jimmy with a yawn. 'What sort of a surprise?'

'That you're not to know. I'm in the secret, of course. But I think you'll like it. It's their own idea entirely.'

'Nice kids,' commented Jimmy tolerantly.

'You're sure you don't mind having them?'

'Not a bit – so long as they don't bother me, they're welcome. After all, they'd nowhere else to go, poor little devils. It was rotten luck their mother dying just before Christmas. I felt very sorry for them.'

Jimmy set down his glass and stretched his legs once more to the blaze.

'Do you know,' said Anne after a pause, 'I think that Derek has a great look of his father.'

'God forbid!' said Jimmy. Then, seeing the look on his wife's face, he added, 'After all, Anne, even if he was your brother, you must admit that Billy was no sort of good.'

Anne was staring into the fire, and her eyes were moist.

'Poor old Billy,' she said. 'Always hard up, always in trouble. The black sheep of the family, even when he was a little boy. I was very fond of him, all the same. And when he died—'

'Now, Anne, you're just being maudlin!'

Anne dabbed at her eyes with a handkerchief.

'I'm sorry,' she said with a gulp. 'I know it's silly of me, but I feel in a way we were responsible.'

'Responsible? For a bomb hitting Eastbury Station? That's a new one on me. I'd always thought it was Hitler who was responsible.'

'I know, but it was our fault that Billy was there, waiting for his train. He wanted to spend the night, and if we'd only let him—'

'Now look here, Anne,' said Jimmy reasonably, 'it's no manner of good getting morbid over what's past and done with. We were neither of us responsible. You were in bed with 'flu – don't you remember? I had to go out on Civil Defence duty – why, I was at Eastbury just after the incident and a nice shambles it was. Billy couldn't have stayed the night, even if I'd have had him – which I wouldn't.'

'I know,' said Anne, miserably, 'I know …'

'Well, let's just forget it, shall we?'

'If only you could forget things by just wanting to—' She pulled herself together. 'Look at the time! I must go and see about getting tea.'

It was with an agreeable feeling of superiority that Jimmy watched her go before he turned back to the fire again. What bundles of nerves women were! Brooding over things that had happened – ten, was it? – no, by Jove, twelve years ago! And all this nonsense about forgetting – you could forget anything if you gave your mind to it, with enough time, and a good digestion and a sensible outlook on life. Anything.

It was a remarkable thing, Jimmy reflected, that until his wife's ill-timed reminiscences had brought it back to his mind he had genuinely forgotten that he had killed his brother-in-law on the night of the raid on Eastbury. And it wasn't just a figure of speech, either. Even with the fellow's son and daughter staying in the house, he had really and truly forgotten what he had done to their father. (Not that it would have made any difference to his treatment of them if he had remembered. It was not their fault, and he bore them no malice.)

He grinned to himself. It *was* pretty extraordinary being able to forget a thing like that. Nobody would believe it if you told them – if you could tell anybody. A pity in a way that you couldn't. It would show some people who always pretended to know everything just how little they knew about human nature. What they didn't understand was that if you had no regrets there was no reason why you should have inconvenient memories. Anne, in her silly fashion, regretted her poor Billy, and that was why she still let her conscience torment her over his death. He had no regrets for that sneaking, blackmailing swine, and consequently no conscience. It was as simple as that.

All the same, thought Jimmy, indulging in the unusual luxury of reminiscence, he had been pretty frightened at the time. But for a marvellous stroke of luck he would never have got away with it. If Jerry hadn't chosen to come over that evening Billy's disappearance would have taken a bit of explaining, and the newly dug patch in the garden looked obvious enough next morning to anyone who cared to make enquiries. But it had all ended happily. Good old Civil Defence! No tiresome inquests in those days. Billy's cigarette case shoved into the pocket of a coat covering a fragment of somebody's carcass had been evidence enough of identity.

As for the other matter, a man could do a lot to a garden in twelve years, with Nature to help him.

In spite of the warmth of the fire, Jimmy found himself shivering. That was what came of remembering things. Now he felt thoroughly upset, all thanks to Anne's stupidity. He picked up his liqueur glass. Empty, of course. Well, there was still time for another drink to set himself up before tea. He made his way to the dining-room.

'Oh, Uncle Jimmy, you oughtn't to have come in!' His niece Tessa looked up at him reproachfully from the floor.

Looking down, Jimmy saw the carpet covered with a mass of shiny objects – silver tinsel, coloured glass balls and miniature wax candles among them.

'What on earth are you up to?' he asked.

'It's your surprise, and now you've spoilt it because it won't be a surprise any more.'

'That's all right,' said Jimmy kindly. I'll look the other way, and forget all about it in no time. I'm awfully good at forgetting.'

He turned to the sideboard and filled his glass. The warm spirit made him feel better again at once. He toasted himself in the looking-glass. 'Here's to forgetting!' he murmured.

He put the glass down, and went through into the kitchen. Anne was buttering slices of bread for tea.

'You oughtn't to have gone in there,' she said.

'So Tessa told me. What is it all about?'

'The children wanted to give you a Christmas tree, to thank you for having them to stay. Isn't it sweet of them? Tessa has been getting all the old decorations out of the attic.'

'Really? That's jolly decent of them. It shows they appreciate things, doesn't it? They've kept it very dark. Where did they hide the tree? I haven't seen it anywhere.'

'I told Derek he could get it out of the garden. You know, that little spruce at the end of the vegetable patch. It's just the right size. You don't mind, do you?'

'D'you mean to say he's cut down the little spruce—?' It was all Jimmy could do not to laugh outright. After what he had been thinking of that afternoon the coincidence seemed irresistibly comic.

'No, dear, not cut down. I knew you wouldn't like that. I told him to dig it up very carefully by the roots, so that we could plant it again. That was all right, wasn't it?'

Jimmy turned and walked out of the room. It was a difficult thing to manage, but he walked. Once out of the house door he ran as he had not run for years. But even as he ran, he knew that it was too late. Fifty yards away he could see the top of the little spruce tremble and sink over to one side, and as he arrived breathless at the spot he saw his nephew standing there, staring incredulously down into the hole where its roots had been.

The Snowball Burglary

H. C. Bailey

A telegram was brought to Mr Fortune. It announced that the woman whom his ingenuity convicted of the Winstanton murder had confessed it in prison just after the Home Secretary decided not to hang her. Mr Fortune sighed satisfaction and took his hostess in to dinner.

He was staying in a Devonshire country house for mental repairs. This is not much like him, for save on visits of duty country houses seldom receive him. The conversation of the county, he complains, is too great a strain upon his intellect. Also, he has no interest in killing creatures, except professionally. But the output of crime had been large that winter and the task of keeping Scotland Yard straight, laborious; and he sought relief with Colonel Beach at Cranston Regis. For Tom Beach, once in the first flight of hunting men, having married a young wife, put central heat and electric light into a remote Tudor manor house, and retired there to grow iris and poultry. Neither poultry nor young wives allured Reggie Fortune, but gardens he loves, and his own iris were not satisfying him.

So he sat by Alice Beach at her table, and while her talk flowed on like the brook in the poem, while he wondered why men marry, since their bachelor dinners are better eating, surveyed with mild eyes her and her guests. Tom Beach had probably been unable to help marrying her, she was so pink and white and round, her eyes so shy and innocent. She was one of those women who make it instantly clear to men that they exist to be married, and Tom Beach has always done his duty. 'But she's not such a fool as she looks,' Reggie had pronounced.

With pity if not sympathy he glanced down the table at Tom Beach, that large, red, honest man who sat doing his best between dignity and impudence, dignity in the awful person of Mrs Faulks and the mighty pretty impudence of his wife's sister, Sally Winslow. Mrs Faulks has been described as one who could never be caught bending, or a model of the art of the corset. She is spare, she is straight; and few have seen her exhibit interest in anything but other people's incomes, which she always distrusts. A correct woman, but for a habit of wearing too many jewels.

What she was doing in Tom Beach's genial house was plain enough. Her son had brought her to inspect Sally Winslow, as a man brings a vet to the horse he fancies. But it was not plain why Alexander Faulks fancied Sally Winslow. Imagine a bulldog after a butterfly. But bulldogs have a sense of humour. Sally Winslow is a wisp of a creature who has no respect for anyone, even herself. Under her bright bobbed hair, indeed, is the daintiest colour; but when some fellow said she had the face of a fairy, a woman suggested the face of a fairy's maid. She listened to Alexander's heavy talk and watched him in a fearful fascination, but sometimes she shot a glance across the table where a little man with a curly head and a roguish eye was eating his dinner demurely. His worst enemies never said that Captain Bunny Cosdon's manners were bad.

Now you know them all. When they made up a four for bridge, upon which Mrs Faulks always insists, it was inevitable that Reggie Fortune should stand out, for his simple mind declines to grasp the principles of cards. Alexander Faulks, in his masterful way, directed Sally to the table; and scared, but submissive, she sat down and giggled nervously. Reggie found himself left to his hostess and Captain Cosdon. They seemed determined to entertain him and he sighed and listened.

So he says. He is emphatic that he did not go to sleep. But the study of the events of that evening which afterwards became necessary, makes it clear that a long time passed before Alice Beach was saying the first thing that he remembers. 'Did you ever know a perfect crime, Mr Fortune?'

Mr Fortune then sat up, as he records, and took notice.

Captain Cosdon burst out laughing, and departed, humming a stave of 'Meet Me Tonight in Dreamland'.

Mr Fortune gazed at his hostess. He had not supposed that she could say anything so sensible. 'Most crimes are perfect,' he said.

'But how horrible! I should hate to be murdered and know there wasn't a clue who did it.'

'Oh, there'll be a clue all right,' Reggie assured her.

'Are you sure? And will you promise to catch my murderer, Mr Fortune?'

'Well, you know,' he considered her round, amiable face, 'if you were murdered it would be a case of art for art's sake. That's very rare. I was speakin' scientifically. A perfect crime is a complete series of cause and effect. Where you have that, there's always a clue, there is always evidence, and when you get to work on it the unknown quantities come out. Yes. Most crimes are perfect. But you must allow for chance. Sometimes the criminal is an idiot. That's a nuisance. Sometimes he has a streak of luck and the crime is damaged before we find it, something has been washed out, a bit of it has been lost. It's the imperfect crimes that give trouble.'

'But how fascinating!'

'Oh, Lord, no,' said Mr Fortune.

The bridge-players were getting up. Sally Winslow was announcing that she had lost all but honour. Mrs Faulks wore a ruthless smile. Sally went off to bed.

'Oh, Mrs Faulks,' her sister cried, 'do come! Mr Fortune is lecturing on crime.'

'Really. How very interesting,' said Mrs Faulks, and transfixed Reggie with an icy stare.

'The perfect criminal in one lesson,' Alice Beach laughed. 'I feel a frightful character already. All you want is luck, you know. Or else Mr Fortune catches you every time.'

'I say, you know, Alice,' her husband protested.

A scream rang out. Alice stopped laughing. The little company looked at each other. 'Where was that?' Tom Beach muttered.

'Not in the house, Colonel,' Faulks said. 'Certainly not in the house.'

Tom Beach was making for the window when all the lights went out.

Alice gave a cry. The shrill voice of Mrs Faulks arose to say, 'Really!' Colonel Beach could be heard swearing. 'Don't let us get excited,' said Faulks. Reggie Fortune struck a match.

'Excited be damned,' said Tom Beach, and rang the bell.

Reggie Fortune, holding his match aloft, made for the door and opened it. The hall was dark, too.

'Oh, Lord, it's the main fuse blown out!' Tom Beach groaned.

'Or something has happened in your little power station,' said Reggie Fortune cheerfully, and his host snorted. For the electricity at Cranston Regis comes from turbines on the stream which used to fill the Tudor fish-ponds, and Colonel Beach loves his machinery like a mother.

He shouted to the butler to bring candles, and out of the dark the voice of the butler was heard apologising. He roared to the chauffeur, who was his engineer, to put in a new fuse. 'It's not the fuse, Colonel,' came a startled voice, 'there's no juice.'

Colonel Beach swore the more. 'Run down to the power-house, confound you. Where the devil are those candles?'

The butler was very sorry, sir, the butler was coming, sir.

'Really!' said Mrs Faulks in the dark, for Reggie had grown tired of striking matches. 'Most inconvenient.' So in the dark they waited ...

And again they heard a scream. It was certainly in the

house this time, it came from upstairs, it was in the voice of Sally Winslow. Reggie Fortune felt someone bump against him, and knew by the weight it was Faulks. Reggie struck another match, and saw him vanish into the darkness above as he called, 'Miss Winslow, Miss Winslow!'

There was the sound of a scuffle and a thud. Colonel Beach stormed upstairs. A placid voice spoke out of the dark at Reggie's ear, 'I say, what's up with the jolly old house?' The butler arrived quivering with a candle in each hand and a bodyguard of candle-bearing satellites, and showed him the smiling face of Captain Cosdon.

From above Colonel Beach roared for lights. 'The C.O. sounds peeved,' said Captain Cosdon. 'Someone's for it, what?'

They took the butler's candles and ran up, discovering with the light Mr Faulks holding his face together. 'Hallo, hallo! Dirty work at the cross-roads, what? Why – Sally! Good God!'

On the floor of the passage Sally Winslow lay like a child asleep, one frail bare arm flung up above her head.

'Look at that. Fortune,' Tom Beach cried. 'Damned scoundrels!'

'Hold the candle,' said Reggie Fortune; but as he knelt beside her the electric light came on again.

'Great Jimmy!' Captain Cosdon exclaimed. 'Who did that?'

'Don't play the fool, Bunny,' Tom Beach growled. 'What have they done to her, Fortune?'

Reggie's plump, capable hands were moving upon the girl delicately. 'Knocked her out,' he said, and stared down at her, and rubbed his chin.

'Who? What? How?' Cosdon cried. 'Hallo, Faulks, what's your trouble? Who hit you?'

'How on earth should I know,' Faulks mumbled, still feeling his face as he peered at the girl. 'When Miss Winslow screamed, I ran up. It was dark, of course. Some men caught hold of me. I struck out and they set on me. I was knocked down. I wish you would look at my eye, Fortune.'

Reggie was looking at Sally, whose face had begun to twitch.

'Your eye will be a merry colour tomorrow,' Cosdon assured him. 'But who hit Sally?'

'It was the fellows who set upon me, I suppose, of course; they were attacking her when I rescued her.'

'Stout fellow,' said Cosdon. 'How many were there?'

'Quite a number. Quite. How can I possibly tell? It was dark. Quite a number.'

Sally tried to sneeze and failed, opened her eyes and murmured, 'The light, the light.' She saw the men about her and began to laugh hysterically.

'Good God, the scoundrels may be in the house still,' cried Tom Beach. 'Come on, Cosdon.'

'I should say so,' said Captain Cosdon, but he lingered over Sally. 'All right now?' he asked anxiously.

'Oh, Bunny,' she choked in her laughter. 'Yes, yes, I'm all right. Oh, Mr Fortune, what is it? Oh, poor Mr Faulks, what has happened?'

'Just so,' said Reggie. He picked her up and walked off with her to her bedroom.

'Oh, you are strong,' she said, not coquetting, but in honest surprise, like a child.

Reggie laughed. 'There's nothing of you,' and he laid her down on her bed. 'Well, what about it?'

'I feel all muzzy.'

'That'll pass off,' said Reggie cheerfully. 'Do you know what hit you?'

'No. Isn't it horrid? It was all dark, you know. There's no end of a bruise.' She felt behind her ear and made a face.

'I know, I know,' Reggie murmured sympathetically. 'And how did it all begin?'

'Why, I came up to bed, Mr Fortune – heavens, there may be a man in here now!' She raised herself.

'Yes, we'd better clear that up,' said Reggie, and looked under the bed and opened the wardrobe and thrust into her dresses and turned back to her. 'No luck, Miss Winslow.'

'Oh, thank goodness,' she sank down again. 'You see, I came up and put the light on, of course, and there was a man at the window there. Then I screamed.'

'The first scream,' Reggie murmured.

'And then the lights went out. I ran away and tumbled over that chair and then out into the passage. I kept bumping into things and it was horrid. And then – oh, somebody caught hold of me and I screamed—'

'The second scream,' Reggie murmured.

'I was sort of flung about. There were men there fighting in the dark. Horrid. Hitting all round me, you know. And then – oh, well, I suppose I stopped one, didn't I?'

There was a tap at the door. 'May I come in, doctor?' said Alice Beach.

'Oh, Alice, have they caught anyone?'

'Not a creature. Isn't it awful? Oh, Sally, you poor darling,' her sister embraced her. 'What a shame! Is it bad?'

'I'm all muddled. And jolly sore.'

'My dear! It is too bad it should be you. Oh, Mr Fortune, what did happen?'

'Some fellow knocked her out. She'll be all right in the morning. But keep her quiet and get her off to sleep.' He went to the window. It was open and the curtains blowing in the wind. He looked out. A ladder stood against the wall. 'And that's that. Yes. Put her to bed, Mrs Beach.'

Outside in the passage he found Captain Cosdon waiting. 'I say, Fortune, is she much hurt?'

'She's taken a good hard knock. She's not made for it. But she'll be all right.'

'Sally! Oh damn,' said Cosdon.

'Did you catch anybody?'

'Napoo. All clear. The Colonel's going round to see if they got away with anything. And Faulks wants you to look at his poor eye.'

'Nothing of yours gone?'

Cosdon laughed. 'No. But I'm not exactly the burglar's friend, don't you know? My family jewels wouldn't please the haughty crook. I say, it's a queer stunt. Ever been in one like it?'

'I don't think it went according to plan,' said Reggie Fortune.

He came down and found Faulks with an eye dwindling behind a bruise of many colours, arguing with an agitated butler that the house must contain arnica. Before he could give the attention which Mr Faulks imperiously demanded, the parade voice of the Colonel rang through the house. 'Fortune, come up here!'

Tom Beach stood in the study where he writes the biographies of his poultry and his iris. There also are kept the cups, medals and other silver with which shows reward their beauty. 'Look at that!' he cried, with a tragic gesture. The black pedestals of the cups, the velvet cases of the medals stood empty.

'Great Jimmy!' said Captain Cosdon in awe.

'Well, that's very thorough,' said Reggie. 'And the next thing, please.'

Colonel Beach said it was a damned outrage. He also supposed that the fellows had stripped the whole place. And he bounced out.

Reggie went to his own room. He had nothing which could be stolen but his brushes, and they were not gone. He looked out of the window. In the cold March moonlight he saw two men moving hither and thither, and recognised one for his chauffeur and factotum Sam, and shouted.

'Nothing doing, sir,' Sam called back. 'Clean getaway.'

Reggie went downstairs to the smoking-room. He was stretched in a chair consuming soda-water and a large cigar when there broke upon him in a wave of chattering Tom Beach and Alice and Captain Cosdon.

'Oh, Mr Fortune, is this a perfect crime?' Alice laughed.

Reggie shook his head. 'I'm afraid it had an accident in its youth. The crime that took the wrong turning.'

'How do you mean, Fortune?' Tom Beach frowned. 'It's deuced awkward.'

'Awkward is the word,' Reggie agreed. 'What's gone, Colonel?'

'Well, there's my pots, you know. And Alice has lost a set of cameos she had in her dressing-room.'

'Pigs!' said Alice with conviction.

'And Mrs Faulks says they've taken that big ruby brooch she was wearing before dinner. You know it.'

'It's one of the things I could bear not to know,' Reggie murmured. 'Nothing else?'

'She says she doesn't know, she's too upset to be sure. I say, Fortune, this is a jolly business for me.'

'My dear chap!'

'She's gone to bed fuming. Faulks is in a sweet state too.'

'What's he lost?'

'Only his eye,' Cosdon chuckled.

'That's the lot, then? Nice little bag, but rather on the small side. Yes, it didn't go according to plan.'

'Oh, Mr Fortune, what are you going to do?'

'Do?' said Reggie reproachfully. 'I? Where's the nearest policeman?'

'Why, here,' Alice pointed at him.

'Cranston Abbas,' said Tom Beach, 'and he's only a yokel. Village constable, don't you know.'

'Yes, you are rather remote, Colonel. What is there about you that brings the wily cracksman down here?'

'Mrs Faulks!' Alice cried. 'That woman must travel with a jeweller's shop. There's a chance for you, Mr Fortune. Get her rubies back and you'll win her heart.'

'Jewelled in fifteen holes. I'd be afraid of burglars. Mrs Beach, you're frivolous, and the Colonel's going to burst into tears. Will anyone tell me what did happen? We were all in the drawing-room — no. Where were you, Cosdon?'

'Writing letters here, old thing.'

'Quite so. And the servants?'

'All in the servants' hall at supper!' Colonel Beach said. 'They are all right.'

'Quite. Miss Winslow went upstairs and saw a man at her window. There's a ladder at it. She screamed and the lights went out. Why?'

'The rascals got at the powerhouse. Baker found the main switch off.'

'Then they knew their way about here. Have you sacked any servant lately? Had any strange workman in the place? No? Yet the intelligence work was very sound. Well, in the darkness Miss Winslow tumbled out into the passage and was grabbed and screamed, and the brave Faulks ran upstairs and took a black eye, and Miss Winslow took the count, and when we arrived there wasn't a burglar in sight. Yes, there was some luck about.'

'Not for Sally,' said her sister.

'No,' said Reggie thoughtfully. 'No, but there was a lot of luck going.' He surveyed them through his cigar smoke with a bland smile.

'What do you think I ought to do, Fortune?' said Tom Beach.

'Go to bed,' said Reggie. 'What's the time? Time runs on, doesn't it? Yes, go to bed.'

'Oh, but, Mr Fortune, you are disappointing,' Alice Beach cried.

'I am. I notice it every day. It's my only vice.'

'I do think you might be interested!'

'A poor crime, but her own,' Captain Cosdon chuckled.

'It's no good, Mrs Beach. It don't appeal to the master mind.'

'You know, Fortune, it's devilish awkward,' the Colonel protested.

'I'm sorry. But what can we do? You might call up your village policeman. He's four miles off, and I dare say he needs exercise. You might telephone to Thorton and say you have been burgled, and will they please watch some road or other for someone or other with a bag of silver and a set of cameos and a ruby brooch. It doesn't sound helpful, does it?'

'It sounds damned silly.'

'But I thought you'd find clues, Mr Fortune,' Alice Beach cried, 'all sorts of clues, fingerprints and footprints and—'

'And tell us the crime was done by a retired sergeant-cook with pink hair and a cast in the eye,' Cosdon grinned.

'You see, I've no imagination,' said Reggie, sadly.

'Confound you, Cosdon, it isn't a joke,' Colonel Beach cried.

'No, I don't think it's a joke,' Reggie agreed.

'One of your perfect crimes, Mr Fortune?'

'Well, I was sayin' – you have to allow for chance. There was a lot of luck about.'

'What are you thinking of?'

'The time, Mrs Beach. Yes, the flight of time. We'd better go to bed.'

But he did not go to bed. He stirred the fire in his bedroom and composed himself by it. The affair annoyed him. He did not want to be bothered by work and his mind insisted on working. Something like this. 'Philosophically time is an illusion. Time travels in divers paces with divers persons.'

Highly divers, yes. Time is the trouble, Colonel. Why was there such a long time between the first scream and the second scream? Sally tumbled down. Sally was fumbling in the dark: but it don't take many minutes to get from her room to the stairs. She took as long as it took the chauffeur to run to the powerhouse. He started some while after the first scream, he had found what was wrong and put the light on again within a minute of the second. Too much time for Sally – and too little. How did Sally's burglars get off so quick? Faulks ran up at the second scream. The rest of us were there next minute. They were there to hit Faulks. When we came, we saw no one, heard no one and found no one.' He shook his head at the firelight. 'And yet Sally's rather a dear. I wonder. No, it didn't go according to plan. But I don't like it, my child. It don't look pretty.'

He sat up. Somebody was moving in the corridor. He went to his table for an electric torch, slid silently across the room, flung open the door and flashed on the light. He caught a glimpse of legs vanishing round a corner, legs which were crawling, a man's legs. A door was closed stealthily.

Reggie swept the light along the floor. It fell at last on some spots of candle grease dropped where the fallen Sally was examined. Thereabouts the legs had been. He moved the light to and fro. Close by stood an old oak settle. He swept the light about it, saw something beneath it flash and picked up Mrs Faulks's big ruby brooch.

The early morning, which he does not love, found him in the garden. There under Sally's window the ladder still stood. 'That came from the potting sheds, sir,' his factotum Sam told him. 'Matter of a hundred yards.'

Together they went over the path and away to the little powerhouse by the stream. The ground was still hard from the night frost.

'Not a trace,' Reggie murmured. 'Well, well. Seen anybody about this morning, Sam?'

'This morning, sir?' Sam stared. 'Not a soul.'

'Have a look,' said Reggie and went in shivering.

He was met by the butler who said nervously that Colonel Beach had been asking for him and would like to see him in the study. There he found not only Colonel Beach but Mrs Beach and Sally and Captain Cosdon, a distressful company. It was plain that Mrs Beach had been crying. Sally was on the brink. Cosdon looked like a naughty boy uncertain of his doom. But the Colonel was tragic, the Colonel was taking things very hard.

Reggie Fortune beamed upon them. 'Morning, morning. Up already, Miss Winslow? How's the head?'

Sally tried to say something and gulped. Tom Beach broke out: 'Sorry to trouble you, Fortune. It's an infernal shame dragging you into this business.' He glared at his wife, and she wilted.

'My dear Colonel, it's my job,' Reggie protested cheerfully, and edged towards the fire which the Colonel screened.

'I'm awfully sorry, Colonel. I'm the one to blame,' Cosdon said. 'It's all my fault, don't you know.'

'I don't know whose fault it isn't. I know it's a most ghastly mess.'

'It's just like a snowball,' Alice laughed hysterically. 'Our snowball burglary.'

'Snowball?' the Colonel roared at her.

'Oh, Tom, you know. When you want subscriptions and have a snowball where everyone has to get someone else to subscribe. I thought of it and I brought in Sally and Sally brought in Bunny and then Mr Faulks came in – poor Mr Faulks – and then Mrs Faulks got into it and her rubies.'

'And now we're all in it, up to the neck.'

'Yes. Yes, that's very lucid,' said Reggie. 'But a little confusing to an outsider. My brain's rather torpid, you know. I only want to get on the fire.' He obtained the central position and sighed happily. 'Well now, the workin' hypothesis is that there were no burglars. Somebody thought it would be interesting to put up a perfect crime. For the benefit of the guileless expert.'

They were stricken by a new spasm of dismay. They stared at him. 'Yes, you always knew it was a fake,' Cosdon cried. 'I guessed that last night when you kept talking about the time.'

'Well, I thought a little anxiety would be good for you. Even the expert has his feelings.'

'It was horrid of us, Mr Fortune,' Sally cried. 'But it wasn't only meant for you.'

'Oh, don't discourage me.'

'It was all my fault, Mr Fortune.' Alice put in her claim and looked at him ruefully and then began to laugh. 'But you did seem so bored—'

'Oh, no, no, no. Only my placid nature. Well now, to begin at the beginning. Somebody thought it would be a merry jest to have me on. That was you, Mrs Beach. For your kindly interest, I thank you.'

Mrs Beach again showed signs of weeping.

'Please don't be horrid, Mr Fortune,' said Sally, fervently.

'I'm trying to be fascinating. But you see I'm so respectable. You unnerve me.'

'I thought of a burglary,' said Mrs Beach, choking sobs. 'And I asked Sally to do it.'

'And she did – all for my sake. Well, one never knows,' Reggie sighed, and looked sentimental.

'It wasn't you,' said Sally. 'I wanted to shock Mr Faulks.'

'Dear, dear. I shouldn't wonder if you have.'

'Oh!' Sally shuddered. 'That man is on my nerves. He simply follows me about. He scares me. When I found he'd got Tom to ask him here I——'

'Yes, of course, it's my fault,' Tom Beach cried. 'I knew it would come round to that.'

'You didn't know, dear, how could you?' Sally soothed him. 'He doesn't make love to you. Well, he was here and his mamma and – oh, Mr Fortune, you've seen them. They want shocking. So I talked to Bunny and——'

'And I came in with both feet,' said Captain Cosdon. 'My scheme really, Fortune, all my scheme.'

'All?' Reggie asked with some emphasis.

'Good Lord, not what's happened.'

'I thought we should come to that some day. What did happen?'

And they all began to talk at once. From which tumult emerged the clear little voice of Sally. 'Bunny slipped out early and put a garden ladder up at my window and then went off to the powerhouse. When I went to bed, I collected Tom's pots from the study – that was because he is so vain of them – and Alice's cameos – that's because they're so dowdy

– and locked them in my trunk. Then I screamed at the window. That was the signal for Bunny and he switched the lights out and came back. All that was what we planned.' She looked pathetically at Reggie. 'It was a good crime, wasn't it, Mr Fortune?'

'You have a turn for the profession, Miss Winslow. You will try to be too clever. It's the mark of the criminal mind.'

'I say, hang it all, Fortune—' Cosdon flushed.

'I know I spoilt it,' said Sally meekly. 'I just stood there, you know, hearing Tom roar downstairs and you all fussing—'

'And you underrate the policeman. Do I fuss?' Reggie was annoyed.

'You're fussing over my morals now. Well, I stood there and it came over me the burglars just had to have something of Mrs Faulks's.' She gurgled. 'That would make it quite perfect. So I ran into her room and struck a match and there was her awful old ruby brooch. I took that and went out into the passage and screamed again. That was the plan. Then I bumped into somebody—'

'That was me,' said Captain Cosdon. 'She was such a jolly long time with the second scream I went up to see if anything was wrong—'

'Yes. The criminal will do too much,' Reggie sighed.

'Then Faulks came. He tumbled into us and hit out, silly ass. I heard Sally go down and I let him have it. Confound him.'

Sally smiled at him affectionately.

'Oh yes, it's devilish funny, isn't it?' cried Tom Beach. 'Good God, Cosdon, you're not fit to be at large. A nice thing you've let me in for.'

'Well, you've all been very ingenious,' said Reggie. 'Thanks for a very jolly evening. May I have some breakfast?' There was a silence which could be felt.

'Mr Fortune,' said Sally, 'that awful brooch is gone.'

'Yes, that's where we slipped up,' said Cosdon. 'Sally must have dropped it when that fool knocked her out. I went out last night to hunt for it and it wasn't there.'

'Really?'

Reggie's tone was sardonic and Cosdon flushed at it. 'What do you mean?'

'Well, somebody found it, I suppose. That's the working hypothesis.'

He reduced them to the dismal condition in which he found them. 'There you are!' Colonel Beach cried. 'Someone of the servants saw the beastly thing and thought there was a chance to steal it. It's a ghastly business. I'll have to go through them for it and catch some poor devil who would have gone straight enough if you hadn't played the fool. It's not fair, confound it.'

There was a tap at the door. Mrs Faulks was asking if the Colonel would speak to her. The Colonel groaned and went out.

'Do you mind if I have some breakfast, Mrs Beach?' said Reggie plaintively.

They seemed to think him heartless but offered no impediment. A dejected company slunk downstairs. It occurred to Reggie, always a just man, that Sam also might be hungry and he ran out to take him off guard.

When he came back to the breakfast-room, he found that Faulks had joined the party. It was clear that no one had dared to tell him the truth. They were gazing in fascinated horror at the many colours which swelled about his right eye, and his scowl was terrible.

'Hallo, Faulks! Stout fellow,' said Reggie, brightly. 'How's the head?'

Mr Faulks turned the scowl on him. Mr Faulks found his head very painful. He had had practically no sleep. He feared some serious injury to the nerves. He must see a doctor. And his tone implied that as a doctor and a man Reggie was contemptible.

Reggie served himself generously with bacon and mushrooms and began to eat. No one else was eating but Mr Faulks. He, in a domineering manner, smote boiled eggs. The others played with food like passengers in a rolling ship.

The door was opened. The austere shape of Mrs Faulks stalked in and behind her Tom Beach slunk to his place. Mrs Faulks's compressed face wore a look of triumph.

Sally half rose from her chair. 'Oh, Mrs Faulks,' she cried, 'have you found your rubies?'

'Really!' said Mrs Faulks with a freezing smile. 'No, Miss Winslow, I have not found my rubies.'

'What are you going to do about it?'

Mrs Faulks stared at her. 'I imagine there is only one thing to be done. I have desired Colonel Beach to send for the police. I should have thought that was obvious.'

'Oh, Tom, you mustn't!' Sally cried.

'Really! My dear, you don't realise what you're saying.'

'Yes, I do. You don't understand, Mrs Faulks; you see it was like this——' and out it all came with the Colonel trying to stop it in confused exclamations, and Mrs Faulks and her heavy son sinking deeper and deeper into stupefaction.

'The whole affair was a practical joke?' said Faulks thickly.

'That's the idea, old thing,' Cosdon assured him.

'Yes, yes, don't you see it?' Sally giggled.

'I never heard anything so disgraceful,' Faulks pronounced.

'I say, go easy,' Cosdon cried.

Mrs Faulks had become pale. 'Am I expected to believe this?' she looked from Tom to Alice.

'Oh, Mrs Faulks, I am so sorry,' Alice Beach said. 'It was too bad. And it's really all my fault.'

'I – I – you say you stole my rubies?' Mrs Faulks turned upon Sally.

'Come, come, the child took them for a joke,' Colonel Beach protested.

'I took them, yes – and then I lost them. I'm most awfully sorry about that.'

'Are you indeed. Am I to believe this tale, Colonel Beach? Then, pray, who stole my diamond necklace?'

She produced an awful silence. She seemed proud of it, and in a fascination of horror the conspirators stared at her.

'Diamond necklace!' Sally cried. 'I never saw it.'

'My necklace is gone. I don't profess to understand the ideas of joking in this house. But my necklace is gone.'

'Oh, my lord,' said Cosdon. 'That's torn it.'

'The snowball!' Alice gasped. 'It is a snowball. Everything gets in something else.'

'Really!' said Mrs Faulks (her one expletive). 'I do not understand you.'

Reggie arose and cut himself a large portion of cold beef.

'If this was a practical joke,' said the solemn voice of Faulks, 'who struck me?'

'That was me, old thing,' Cosdon smiled upon him.

'But strictly speakin',' said Reggie as he came back and took more toast, 'that's irrelevant.'

'Colonel Beach!' Mrs Faulks commanded the wretched man's attention, 'what do you propose to do?'

'We shall have to have the police,' he groaned.

'Oh, yes, it's a case for the police,' said Reggie cheerfully. 'Have you a telegraph form, Colonel?'

'It's all right, Fortune, thanks. I'll telephone.'

'Yes, encourage local talent. But I would like to send a wire to Scotland Yard.'

'Scotland Yard!' Mrs Faulks was impressed. Mrs Faulks smiled on him.

'Well, you know, there are points about your case, Mrs Faulks. I think they would be interested.'

Like one handing his own death warrant, Colonel Beach put down some telegraph forms. Reggie pulled out his pencil, laid it down again and took some marmalade. 'Valuable necklace, of course, Mrs Faulks?' he said blandly. 'Quite so. The one you wore the night before last? I remember. I remember.' He described it. Mrs Faulks approved and elaborated his description. 'That's very clear. Are your jewels insured? Yes, well, that is a certain consolation.' He adjusted his pencil and wrote. 'I think this will meet the case.' He gave the telegram to Mrs Faulks.

Mrs Faulks read it, Mrs Faulks seemed unable to

understand. She continued to gaze at it, and the wondering company saw her grow red to the frozen coils of her hair.

Reggie was making notes on another telegraph form. He read out slowly a precise description of the lost necklace. 'That's it, then,' he said. 'By the way, who are you insured with?'

Mrs Faulks glared at him. 'I suppose this is another joke.'

'No,' Reggie shook his head. 'This has gone beyond a joke.'

'Where is my brooch, then? Who has my brooch?'

'I have,' said Reggie. He pulled it out of his pocket and laid it on her plate. 'I found the brooch in the passage. I didn't find the necklace, Mrs Faulks. So I should like to send that telegram.'

'You will do nothing of the kind. I won't have anything done. The whole affair is disgraceful, perfectly disgraceful. I forbid you to interfere. Do you understand, I forbid it? Colonel Beach! It is impossible for me to stay in your house after the way in which you have allowed me to be treated. Please order the car.'

She stalked out of the room.

'Fortune!' said Faulks thunderously. 'Will you kindly explain yourself?'

'I don't think I need explaining. But you might ask your mother. She kept the telegram.' And to his mother Mr Faulks fled.

'Good God, Fortune, what have you done?' Tom Beach groaned.

'Not a nice woman,' said Reggie sadly. 'Not really a nice woman.' He stood up and sought the fire and lit a cigar and sighed relief.

'Mr Fortune, what was in that telegram?' Sally cried.

Reggie sat down on the cushioned fender. 'I don't think you're really a good little girl, you know,' he shook his head at her and surveyed the company. 'Broadly speakin' you ought all to be ashamed of yourselves. Except the Colonel.'

'Please, Mr Fortune, I'll never do it again,' said Alice plaintively. 'Tom—' She sat on the arm of her husband's chair and caressed him.

'All right, all right,' he submitted. 'But I say, Fortune, what am I to do about Mrs Faulks?'

'She's done all there is to do. No, not a nice woman.'

Sally held out her small hands. 'Please! What did you say in that telegram?'

'"Lomas, Scotland Yard. Jewel robbery Colonel Beach's house curious features tell post office stop delivery registered packet posted Cranston this morning nine examine contents Reginald Fortune Cranston Regis."'

'I don't understand.'

'She did. Sorry to meddle with anyone in your house. Colonel. But she would have it. You won't have any trouble.'

'But what's the woman done?' the Colonel cried.

'Well, you know, she's been led into temptation. When she thought burglars had taken her brooch it seemed to her that she might as well recover from the insurance people for something else too. That's the worst of playing at crime, Mrs Beach. You never know who won't take it seriously. What made me cast an eye at Mrs Faulks was her saying last night that she wasn't sure whether she had lost anything else. I can't imagine Mrs Faulks not sure about anything. She's sure she's an injured woman now. And I'll swear she always has an inventory of all her jeweller's shop in her head.'

'She has,' said Alice Beach pathetically. 'You should hear her talk of her jewels.'

'Heaven forbid. But you see, Miss Winslow, it's the old story, you criminals always try to be too clever. She thought it wouldn't be enough to say she'd lost her diamonds. She wanted them well out of the way so that the police could search and not find them. So she scurried off to the post office and sent them away in a registered packet. Thus, as you criminals will, underratin' the intelligence of the simple policeman. My man Sam was looking out to see if anyone did anything unusual this morning and he observed Mrs Faulks's manoeuvres at the post office—'

'And you had her cold!' Cosdon cried.

'Yes. Yes, a sad story.'

'She didn't really mean any harm,' said Sally. 'Did she, Mr Fortune?'

Reggie looked at her sadly. 'You're not a moral little girl, you know,' he said.

Tall Story

Margery Allingham

London was having one of her days. Outside, the streets glistened dully with half-frozen sludge and the air was thick, dark and apparently contaminated with poison gas. But inside the varnished cabin which overhung the huge circular bar of the Platelayers' Arms, W.2, there was still civilisation and comfort. In this nest which possessed a staircase direct to the street, privileged customers drank in all the peaceful privacy of a St James's Club yet without sacrificing anything of the fug and freedom of the true hostelry. Mrs Chubb, the licensee, who was a genius in such matters called it 'my little room'.

Charlie Luke, at that time the Divisional Detective Chief Inspector of the district, was sitting on the table, his muscles spoiling the cut of his jacket and his hat pulled down over his eyes. He looked like a gangster, was a tough, and with his live dark face and diamond-shaped eye sockets, he lent a touch of badly needed theatre to the rest of us. We were about half a dozen I suppose, no one of staggering distinction but all friends, resting for half an hour before making the routine after-work effort to totter off home.

Mr Campion, owlish behind the spectacles for which he had set such a fashion, was chipping Luke gently and affectionately like a man knocking out a favourite pipe. 'You put your success as a detective down to your height, Charles?' he was saying. 'Really? You astound me. I shouldn't have thought it. Height of brow? Or merely length of leg?'

'Reach, chum.' Luke was in fine ferocious form, his eyes snapping and his teeth gleaming in his dark skin. 'And I wasn't talking of my success – I could do with a basinful of that – I simply said that it was my height that got me into the C.I.D. I was on the beat – see?'

He adjusted an imaginary helmet strap under his chin and strained his Adam's apple against an imaginary tunic collar. He was away. You could see him fifteen years younger, with pink satin cheeks, loping along, bright, eager, green as lettuce leaves. It was his great gift, as he spoke whole pictures came alive and people one had never heard of seemed to step into the room. Mr Campion settled back, grinning.

'It was a night just like this, cold and thick as a landlady's kiss and my little beat, which was usually quiet at night except for the rats, had come alive for a change. Our D.I. was expecting a burglary.'

He blew out his cheeks, sketched himself a pair of flaring eyebrows and a waterfall moustache with a careless hand and sped on with his narrative, having introduced us to a fussy, worried personality without drawing extra breath.

'Set out!' he said. 'Caudblimeah! I thought he was expecting to be a father until seven in the evening when the cars turned out! My sergeant took pity on me in the end and gave it me in clear. News had come through on the grapevine that Slacks Washington, who was one of the slicker practitioners, had run out of money and had been taking sights round a little bookmaker's office in Ebury Court. From information received – and you know what that means ...' he favoured us with a wide-eyed leer which was somehow wholly feminine and conjured up a traitress of a very definite kind ... 'they'd learned that tonight was the night. The bookie kept his cash in a safe which wouldn't keep out pussy and he was careless. He relied on the position of the office.'

There was a square whisky bottle on the mantelshelf – a dummy, as many generations of Ma Chubb's clients had discovered through the years; Luke leant forward without rising and, stretching out a long arm, took it up with which to demonstrate.

'This is just about the shape of Ebury Court,' he remarked, placing the bottle on its side. 'There's a narrow tunnelled entrance off the Commercial Road, two perfectly blank thirty-foot walls made of soot-blackened brick, smarmed with posters, and, at the end, here at the bottom of the bottle, is a little nest of offices. A small printery on the ground floor, the bookie above and a commercial art studio above that ... nothing to attract anybody. All deserted at night.'

He grinned at us. 'They could have cut short the whole exercise by just putting me in the passageway,' he said cheerfully. 'Naturally. But our D.I. wasn't wasting anything. Slacks was two and one-sixth yards of ill repute at that time.

He was tall and thin and dangerous, he used a gun, he was dirty and he stole.' He measured two yards in the air as a woman does with outstretched arm and held his nose for a moment. 'A *bad* crook,' he said. 'So it was decided to take him with the stuff on him just to make a nice clean open-and-shut case which no smarty legal-eagle could muck up. It was also to be an object lesson to a collection of new young gentlemen from the C.I.D. (at that time of day, half the stuff they were recruiting spoke so refined their superior officers couldn't understand a word they were saying) and old Superintendent Yeo from the Yard was to be present himself just to hand out the congratulations.' He laughed joyfully. 'Talk about a police-net!' he said. 'The trouble was to prevent it looking like a football crowd caught in the rain. I was the only man allowed to show myself. I was to keep my usual times and "behave normal" and I was just bright enough to know that didn't mean stopping in a doorway for a fag.

'Off we went. There were police in the area, police on the tiles, police disguised as disappointed lovers waiting for their girls, police disguised as drunks singing in the gutter, police disguised as postmen, police disguised as police going home.' He crossed his eyes and his fingers and made an idiot face. 'It was quite a do,' he said. 'It was a wonder to me Slacks pushed past 'em all. There was no one else about. There never were many people around at that time of night, but the rain and the fog seemed to have cleared the district. By midnight I'd given up hope, but at a quarter to one he showed up. He got off a bus on the corner, leaving the man who was tailing him to ride on as arranged, and came striding down the pavement with his raincoat flapping and his long legs making shadows on the pavement under the street lamp. I recognised him at once from the pictures I'd been shown. He saw me and said, "Good night, officer!" as he passed. He was so much at ease that it was me that gave the guilty start. I made a police-like noise and strolled on – you know.' The D.D.C.I. rubbed his cheek and miraculously we saw him as he must have been then, skin like pink satin and the kitten-blue still in his eyes.

'Slacks went into the trap,' he went on. 'Walked straight into the Court like a man in a hurry, which was the only way; the dark mouth of the tunnel through the houses swallowed him up and after that you could have heard a cat cough.

'It had been arranged that the arrest should be made as he came out of Ebury Court. The idea was that since he was known to be dangerous the actual cop should be covered at all points. It was to be a demonstration, as I said. The whole thing was to be done like the book, neat, swift and with the minimum danger to all present. Since I'd done my little bit, I walked back when I reached the boundary and crossed the road to see the performance.

'There it was, set out like a stage set. There was a man on either side of the entrance waiting to step forward and pin him. There was a car twenty paces up the road and another one thirty paces down, stationary but with engines running. Opposite, there was a borrowed G.P.O. van with two fake postmen in attendance, and all round – hidden, they hoped, in the dusk and weather – there were the privileged audience. We waited. We waited. We waited some more. People began to get windy. There had been time for

Slacks to open twenty safes and count the money as well. I could feel our D.I. shaking although he was forty yards away. I know what he felt like. But I was puzzled myself because I knew there was no other way out and the roofs were manned. I found myself wondering if the chap could have broken his leg or something, knocked himself out, perhaps, with the bookie's Scotch. And then quite suddenly, between thought and thought as it were, with no one quite ready in spite of everything, a revolver shot rang out clearly from inside the Court. There was a yelp like the cry of a lost soul (whatever that's like) and someone came staggering out into the street.

'I saw him and I recognised him and I had the shock of my life. The men on the tunnel caught him and he collapsed in their arms and died there, poor chap, at that moment, with a bullet through his windpipe.

'I was one of the first to get there, although there was soon a big enough crowd round the three of them.

'The D.I. charged up spluttering' — Luke blew the imaginary waterfall moustache in and out until we saw it for ourselves — 'he kept the watch on the archway intact, though; he was no fool, the Old Man. He turned to me. "Who the so-and-so is this, constable?" he demanded, as suspiciously as if he thought it was all mine. "Know him?"

'I said, "Yessir!" smartly, and I told him. It was a little runt called Church — some relation to the proverbial mouse, I think — he was a crank who spent all his spare time fly-posting for some society he was interested in. I always remember those little posters of his, they were printed in emerald on yellow and he stuck them wherever he could on the hoardings, quite illegally. They said: "YOU'VE GOT A RIGHT TO IT", and then, in some very small type: *Society of Humanity. Meeting Tuesday. Somewhereorother Hall.* That was all. The most innocent little chap alive. I went to one of the meetings once, but it emerged that the only thing I'd got a right to was the speaker's views and they didn't get me far. Church was daft, that was all. A poor daft little bloke. He must have been hiding in the Court for hours – thinking all the ding-dong was for him, I suppose.

'We could see what had happened. He'd surprised Slacks and got the full benefit. Strewth I was riled!' Even at this distance in time the D.D.C.I.'s diamond-shaped eyes grew narrow at the recollection. 'I was all for charging in like a hero and getting the next bullet,' he said with a lightning change of mood. 'Mercifully I had no enemies among my superiors at that time and I was restrained. We all waited there till morning. Finally, after sufficient conferences to start a Peace, old D.I. Everett himself went in. God bless him he was a brave old boy. He had a bullet-proof shirt on, so his tummy was safe but the etiquette of the time required him to rely on the natural armour plating of his own skull should Slacks have aimed high. He had four of his own boys behind him but I got there next, there being no great competition.

'We found Slacks sitting on a packing-case outside the printery, smoking and admiring the view. He was quite affable, all things considered.'

Luke paused and eyed Campion.

'You ought to have been there,' he said. 'It was like one of your tame pidgins. The crib was cracked, the cash was gone, Church's little paste-pot and Escapist Literature were lying in the yard, but Slacks hadn't a bob on him and nor had he a gun.

'Everett's men took the whole place apart. It was the first time I'd ever seen a full-dress C.I.D. search and it opened my eyes. They took up the drains, although anyone could see they hadn't been disturbed for twenty years, they took the offices apart, they tapped the stones and the walls and they emptied the paste-pot — so it wasn't what you're thinking — and meanwhile Slacks sat placidly in a nice warm room overlooking the river and swore he couldn't think what they were all talking about and hadn't heard a shot or even handled a gun whatever next.

'No one told me to go off duty so I stayed around. When they were all exhausted and the place looked like the scoured inside of a well-kept saucepan, the C.I.D. boys were called off. The old D.I. was nearly out of his mind. He was standing alone in the middle of the court with the sun shining down through the air-shaft between the building and glinting on his old bald head. The bookie and the printers and the commercial artists were all besieging the entrance behind us and he knew that sooner or later he'd have to let them in and lose the proof for ever.

'Since there was no one else there he spoke to me. "Where did he put it, constable?" he said. "Where in the name of Gog and Magog did he put that gun — the gun and wad of money as big as a brick?"

'I cleared my throat — I was a bit husky when speaking to D.I.s in those days. "He's a tall man, sir," I said.

'He turned and looked at me and I remember I took my cape off and stretched up my hand — my reach was eight inches longer than his own. "Church was a little man, sir," I said and I pointed to one of the "YOU'VE GOT A RIGHT TO IT" posters, which was a good two feet higher than the rest, slapped on in the very midst of an out-of-date Cinema Masterpiece which covered half a wall. He opened his mouth and said a word which was new to me – Hindustani it was. He was an elderly man. He went over and reached up. He wasn't tall enough, but I waited for orders and saw the look on his face when he gave them.'

Luke sighed and on his dark face there was a gleam of remembered triumph. 'It was there,' he said. 'In a little hole made by the erosion of a couple of bricks. The bill posters always papered over it, but within a day or so the paper always rotted. Slacks, looking round wildly after the shot, must have guessed that he was trapped. He saw the hole, shoved the loot and the gun out of sight, and then spotted the paste-pot and the bills.

'I remember the D.I. holding the stuff in his handkerchief. He was grinning all over his face, like this' – Luke's smile was wonderful to see. '"You think I'm going to take the credit for this, my boy, don't you?" he said. I said, "Yessir," and he laughed. "How right you are," he said. "Learnt anything?" I said: "Yessir, always take the paper off the wall, sir." That made him laugh. "You'll do," he said. "You'd better report to me." So that's how I joined the C.I.D.'

Mr Campion was laughing.

'Brilliant observation,' he remarked. 'And – er – if I may say so, wonderful restraint.'

Luke chuckled, and appealed to the rest of us.

'He always spots the second degree,' he said. 'Yes, of

course you're right, chum! I saw it at once as soon as I stepped into the yard. That hole in the wall was where I kept my sandwiches. It was just high enough to be private. All the same I had to wait my moment – "Honour where honour is going to be duly appreciated".'

A Present from Santa Claus

Julian Symons

'I want to see Santa Claus,' said Francis Quarles's nephew Jonathan. 'Will he give me a present?'

'I expect so.' They stood in the toy department of Merridge's among other late shoppers, on Christmas Eve. Children were experimenting with space pistols while their fathers longingly fingered electric trains. Balsa wood boomerangs curved gracefully through the air, monkeys performed trapeze acts over and over again, a woman demonstrator blew balloons out of the most unlikely looking material.

At one end of the department a sign said: 'Children. Enter Aladdin's Cave and get your present from Santa Claus himself. One shilling only.' A queue of children went in by the pay desk and came out holding small parcels wrapped in bright paper. Most looked delighted, one or two were snivel-ling, a small boy with fair hair swung his blue paper parcel by its tinsel string with an air of boredom.

It was a cheerful scene, but Sir Wilfred Merridge, who had been showing Quarles round the store, looked worried. He began to talk about the thefts at Merridge's. 'They began a fortnight ago as petty pilfering, but now they've gone far beyond that. At first it was fountain pens, scarves, cigar cutters, that kind of thing. Yesterday we lost a brooch worth eight guineas, an expensive bottle of perfume and a diamond-studded wristwatch among other things. More than fifty pounds' worth of stuff altogether.'

'And you're sure it's someone who works here, not customers?'

'Too regular for ordinary shop thefts. It happens every day. Must be a little gang among the temporary staff engaged for Christmas. It's not difficult to steal things, mark you. What we can't understand – my word, what's that?'

'You're dead,' said Jonathan Quarles triumphantly. He had pushed into Sir Wilfred's back an oddly shaped red plastic instrument which screeched when he pressed a button. 'Can I have this, Uncle Francis? It's a rocket detonator with atomic flame.'

Quarles paid a beaming assistant. Sir Wilfred resumed. 'What I can't understand is how they get the stuff out. I've had four times our usual staff of detectives keeping watch these last few days and they're convinced it's not passed to customer accomplices. And the staff don't go out in the daytime. We've got a canteen which everybody uses at this time of year when the lunch hour has to be short. For the last three nights we've asked all the staff to submit to a search before leaving – purely voluntary, of course. We found nothing.'

'*When* can I get a present from Santa Claus, Uncle Francis?'

'In a minute. Go and look at the railway trains and see if you can buy a level crossing or signals or something that doesn't cost more than ten shillings.'

When Jonathan had rushed away with the note in his hand Quarles said: 'What's to stop the thieves from passing things to other members of the staff in the canteen?'

'They could do that, but it still leaves the problem of how they get the stuff out. If there were accomplice customers, our detectives would have noticed them hanging round one department or another. They've been watching particularly for anything like that.'

'Trivial, but teasing,' Quarles said. 'What kind of size were the things stolen?'

'Small things, almost all of them. The biggest was a pair of solid silver candlesticks. If you're thinking of anything like secret pockets in clothing, I can assure you—'

'Nothing like that,' Quarles said absently. 'I say, whatever has that nephew of mine got now?'

'Here's something much better than signals and level crossings.' Jonathan Quarles took out of a cardboard box a bright green parrot, wound it up and placed it on a counter nearby. The bird immediately began to flap its wings up and down and move along the counter squawking: 'I've lost my buttons and braces. Hey, damn your eyes.' Jonathan's own eyes were bright with delight. 'Isn't it supersonic, Uncle Francis? Can I have it?'

'Certainly, my boy. Just the thing to appeal to your grandmother. Ask the assistant to wrap it up.'

'And *can* I see Santa Claus?'

'As soon as you've got that bird wrapped up.' He turned again to Sir Wilfred. 'Is it literally true that everybody is searched?'

'Certainly.'

'Are you searched, for example?'

Sir Wilfred went very red. 'Of course not. Should I steal my own property?'

'I don't suppose so. I only wanted to point out that when you said everybody had been searched it wasn't literally true. In the same way your store detectives looked out for customers coming in contact with the staff, but I doubt if they thought of—'

'Can I see Santa Claus and get my present now?'

'Yes, you can.' Quarles gave Jonathan a shilling. He paid it at the desk and joined the now dwindling queue. 'What kind of things do they get?' Quarles asked.

'Little clockwork toys, cardboard cut-outs, that kind of thing. Splendid value. They cost us more than a shilling, but we do it to keep the youngsters happy.' And to keep them in the Toy Department, Quarles reflected. Sir Wilfred said impatiently: 'You've got nothing practical to suggest, then?'

'I'm not sure. Here he comes.' Behind the curtains they heard Jonathan pipe: 'Merry Christmas,' and the answering boom of Santa Claus: 'And a Merry Christmas to you, my boy.'

*

Jonathan came out carrying a little box. Behind him came a small fair-haired boy who swung his green paper parcel by its tinsel string with an air of boredom. 'That's the boy,' Quarles said. He put a large hand on the fair-haired boy's shoulder. 'Let's see what Santa Claus has given you.'

'Let me go.' The boy wriggled furiously but Quarles held him comfortably with one hand and tore off the parcel's paper wrapping to reveal a gleaming cigarette case.

Sir Wilfred gave an outraged exclamation and picked it up. 'Solid silver. The little scoundrel.'

Jonathan, who had undone his own parcel, said: 'That's much better than mine. I've only got a jigsaw puzzle.'

The boy suddenly raised his voice to a shout. 'Bill, they've got me.'

A moment later surprised shoppers in Merridge's saw Santa Claus emerge from behind his curtain and run as quickly as his long red cloak would permit across the room. At the department entrance two unobtrusive men gripped him by the arms.

'It was absurdly simple,' Quarles said, with a touch of mock modesty. 'Probably there were four of them in it. Is that right?' he asked the boy.

'Yes. Bill's wife got a job in cosmetics and Harry Jones is in jewellery.'

'They stole the things and passed them on to Santa Claus in the canteen at lunchtime. He handed them out as presents to this boy – the kind of customer your detectives never noticed coming into contact with the staff. I realised what was happening when I saw him going in three times in a few minutes. Not even your presents are such good value as that.'

'Most observant.' Sir Wilfred seemed quite overwhelmed. 'I don't know how to thank you. Your fee—'

'No fee. I have only one request to make. When you've got the stolen things back, don't make a charge.' Quarles released his grip on the fair boy and ran a hand through his nephew's hair. 'After all, it *is* Christmas Eve.'

The Undignified Melodrama of the Bone of Contention

Dorothy L. Sayers

'I am afraid you have brought shocking weather with you, Lord Peter,' said Mrs Frobisher-Pym, with playful reproof. 'If it goes on like this they will have a bad day for the funeral.'

Lord Peter Wimsey glanced out of the morning-room window to the soaked green lawn and the shrubbery, where the rain streamed down remorselessly over the laurel leaves, stiff and shiny like mackintoshes.

'Nasty exposed business, standing round at funerals,' he agreed.

'Yes, I always think it's such a shame for the old people. In a tiny village like this it's about the only pleasure they get during the winter. It makes something for them to talk about for weeks.'

'Is it anybody's funeral in particular?'

'My dear Wimsey,' said his host, 'it is plain that you, coming from your little village of London, are quite out of the swim. There has never been a funeral like it in Little Doddering before. It's an event.'

'Really?'

'Oh dear, yes. You may possibly remember old Burdock?'

'Burdock? Let me see. Isn't he a sort of local squire, or something?'

'He was,' corrected Mr Frobisher-Pym. 'He's dead – died in New York about three weeks ago, and they're sending him over to be buried. The Burdocks have lived in the big house for hundreds of years, and they're all buried in the church-yard, except, of course, the one who was killed in the War. Burdock's secretary cabled the news of his death across, and said the body was following as soon as the embalmers had finished with it. The boat gets in to Southampton this morning, I believe. At any rate, the body will arrive here by the 6.30 from Town.'

'Are you going down to meet it, Tom?'

'No, my dear. I don't think that is called for. There will be a grand turn-out of the village, of course. Joliffe's people are having the time of their lives; they borrowed an extra pair of horses from young Mortimer for the occasion. I only hope they don't kick over the traces and upset the hearse. Mortimer's horseflesh is generally on the spirited side.'

'But, Tom, we must show some respect to the Burdocks.'

'We're attending the funeral tomorrow, and that's quite enough. We must do that, I suppose, out of consideration for the family, though, as far as the old man himself goes, respect is the very last thing anybody would think of paying him.'

'Oh, Tom, he's dead.'

'And quite time too. No, Agatha, it's no use pretending that old Burdock was anything but a spiteful, bad-tempered, dirty-living old blackguard that the world's well rid of. The last scandal he stirred up made the place too hot to hold him. He had to leave the country and go to the States, and, even so, if he hadn't had the money to pay the people off, he'd probably have been put in gaol. That's why I'm so annoyed with Hancock. I don't mind his calling himself a priest, though clergyman was always good enough for dear old Weeks – who, after all, was a canon – and I don't mind his vestments. He can wrap himself up in a Union Jack if he likes – it doesn't worry *me*. But when it comes to having old Burdock put on trestles in the south aisle, with candles round him, and Hubbard from the "Red Cow" and Duggins's boy praying over him half the night, I think it's time to draw the line. The people don't like it, you know – at least, the older generation don't. It's all right for the young ones, I dare say; they must have their amusement; but it gives offence to a lot of the farmers. After all, they knew Burdock a bit too well. Simpson – he's people's warden, you know – came up quite in distress to speak to me about it last night. You couldn't have a sounder man than Simpson. I said I would speak to Hancock. I did speak to him this morning, as a matter of fact, but you might as well talk to the west door of the church.'

'Mr Hancock is one of those young men who fancy they know everything,' said his wife. 'A sensible man would have listened to you, Tom. You're a magistrate and have lived here all your life, and it stands to reason you know considerably more about the parish than he does.'

'He took up the ridiculous position,' said Mr Frobisher-Pym, 'that the more sinful the old man had been the more he needed praying for. I said, "I think it would need more praying than you or I could do to help old Burdock out of the place he's in now." Ha, ha! So he said, "I agree with you, Mr Frobisher-Pym; that is why I am having eight watchers to pray all through the night for him." I admit he had me there.'

'Eight people?' exclaimed Mrs Frobisher-Pym.

'Not all at once, I understand; in relays, two at a time. "Well," I said, "I think you ought to consider that you will be giving a handle to the Nonconformists." Of course, he couldn't deny that.'

Wimsey helped himself to marmalade. Nonconformists, it seemed, were always searching for handles. Though what kind – whether door-handles, tea-pot handles, pump-handles, or starting-handles – was never explained, nor what the handles were to be used for when found. However, having been brought up in the odour of the Establishment, he was familiar with this odd dissenting peculiarity, and merely said:

'Pity to be extreme in a small parish like this. Disturbs the ideas of the simple fathers of the hamlet and the village blacksmith, with his daughter singin' in the choir and the Old Hundredth and all the rest of it. Don't Burdock's family have anything to say to it? There are some sons, aren't there?'

'Only the two, now. Aldine was the one that was killed, of course, and Martin is somewhere abroad. He went off after that row with his father, and I don't think he has been back in England since.'

'What was the row about?'

'Oh, that was a disgraceful business. Martin got a girl into trouble – a film actress or a typist or somebody of that sort – and insisted on marrying her.'

'Oh?'

'Yes, so dreadful of him,' said the lady, taking up the tale, 'when he was practically engaged to the Delaprime girl – the one with glasses, you know. It made a terrible scandal. Some horribly vulgar people came down and pushed their way into the house and insisted on seeing old Mr Burdock. I will say for him he stood up to them – he wasn't the sort of person you could intimidate. He told them the girl had only herself to blame, and they could sue Martin if they liked – *he* wouldn't be blackmailed on his son's account. The butler was listening at the door, naturally, and told the whole village about it. And then Martin Burdock came home and had a quarrel with his father you could have heard for miles. He said that the whole thing was a lie, and that he meant to marry the girl, anyway. I cannot understand how anybody could marry into a blackmailing family like that.'

'My dear,' said Mr Frobisher-Pym gently, 'I don't think you're being quite fair to Martin, or his wife's parents, either. From what Martin told me, they were quite decent people, only not his class, of course, and they came in a well-meaning way to find out what Martin's "intentions" were. You would want to do the same yourself, if it were a daughter of ours. Old Burdock, naturally, thought they meant blackmail. He was the kind of man who thinks everything can be paid for; and he considered a son of his had a perfect right to seduce a young woman who worked for a living. I don't say Martin was altogether in the right—'

'Martin is a chip off the old block, I'm afraid,' retorted the lady. 'He married the girl, anyway, and why should he do that, unless he had to?'

'Well, they've never had any children, you know,' said Mr Frobisher-Pym.

'That's as may be. I've no doubt the girl was in league with her parents. And you know the Martin Burdocks have lived in Paris ever since.'

'That's true,' admitted her husband. 'It was an unfortunate affair altogether. They've had some difficulty in tracing Martin's address, too, but no doubt he'll be coming back shortly. He is engaged in producing some film play, they tell me, so possibly he can't get away in time for the funeral.'

'If he had any natural feeling, he would not let a film play stand in his way,' said Mrs Frobisher-Pym.

'My dear, there are such things as contracts, with very heavy monetary penalties for breaking them. And I don't suppose Martin could afford to lose a big sum of money. It's not likely that his father will have left him anything.'

'Martin is the younger son, then?' asked Wimsey, politely showing more interest than he felt in the rather well-worn plot of this village melodrama.

'No, he is the eldest of the lot. The house is entailed, of course, and so is the estate, such as it is. But there's no money in the land. Old Burdock made his fortune in rubber shares during the boom, and the money will go as he leaves it – wherever that may be, for they haven't found any will yet. He's probably left it all to Haviland.'

'The younger son?'

'Yes. He's something in the City – a director of a company – connected with silk stockings, I believe. Nobody has seen very much of him. He came down as soon as he heard of his father's death. He's staying with the Hancocks. The big house has been shut up since old Burdock went to the States four years ago. I suppose Haviland thought it wasn't worth while opening it up till they knew what Martin was going to do about it. That's why the body is being taken to the church.'

'Much less trouble, certainly,' said Wimsey.

'Oh, yes – though, mind you, I think Haviland ought to take a more neighbourly view of it. Considering the position the Burdocks have always held in the place, the people had a right to expect a proper reception after the funeral. It's usual. But these business people think less of tradition than we do down here. And, naturally, since the Hancocks are putting Haviland up, he can't raise much objection to the candles and the prayers and things.'

'Perhaps not,' said Mrs Frobisher-Pym, 'but it would have been more suitable if Haviland had come to us, rather than to the Hancocks, whom he doesn't even know.'

'My dear, you forget the very unpleasant dispute I had with Haviland Burdock about shooting over my land. After the correspondence that passed between us, last time he was down here, I could scarcely offer him hospitality. His father took a perfectly proper view of it, I will say that for him, but Haviland was exceedingly discourteous to me, and things were said which I could not possibly overlook. However, we mustn't bore you, Lord Peter, with our local small-talk. If you've finished your breakfast, what do you say to a walk round the place? It's a pity it's raining so hard – and you don't see the garden at its best this time of the year, of course – but I've got some cocker spaniels you might like to have a look at.'

Lord Peter expressed eager anxiety to see the spaniels, and in a few minutes' time found himself squelching down the gravel path which led to the kennels.

'Nothing like a healthy country life,' said Mr Frobisher-Pym. 'I always think London is so depressing in the winter. Nothing to do with one's self. All right to run up for a day or two and see a theatre now and again, but how you people stick it week in and week out beats me. I must speak to Plunkett about this archway,' he added. 'It's getting out of trim.'

He broke off a dangling branch of ivy as he spoke. The plant shuddered revengefully, tipping a small shower of water down Wimsey's neck.

The cocker spaniel and her family occupied a comfortable and airy stall in the stable buildings. A youngish man in breeches and leggings emerged to greet the visitors, and produced the little bundles of puppyhood for their inspection. Wimsey sat down on an upturned bucket and examined them gravely one by one. The bitch, after cautiously reviewing his boots and grumbling a little, decided that he was trustworthy and slobbered genially over his knees.

'Let me see,' said Mr Frobisher-Pym, 'how old are they?'

'Thirteen days, sir.'

'Is she feeding them all right?'

'Fine, sir. She's having some of the malt food. Seems to suit her very well, sir.'

'Ah, yes. Plunkett was a little doubtful about it, but I heard it spoken very well of. Plunkett doesn't care for experiments, and, in a general way, I agree with him. Where is Plunkett, by the way?'

'He's not very well this morning, sir.'

'Sorry to hear that, Merridew. The rheumatics again?'

'No, sir. From what Mrs Plunkett tells me, he's had a bit of a shock.'

'A shock? What sort of a shock? Nothing wrong with Alf or Elsie, I hope?'

'No, sir. The fact is – I understand he's seen something, sir.'

'What do you mean, seen something?'

'Well, sir – something in the nature of a warning, from what he says.'

'A warning? Good heavens, Merridew, he mustn't get those sort of ideas in his head. I'm surprised at Plunkett; I always thought he was a very level-headed man. What sort of warning did he say it was?'

'I couldn't say, sir.'

'Surely he mentioned what he thought he'd seen.'

Merridew's face took on a slightly obstinate look.

'I can't say, I'm sure, sir.'

'This will never do. I must go and see Plunkett. Is he at the cottage?'

'Yes, sir.'

'We'll go down there at once. You don't mind, do you, Wimsey? I can't allow Plunkett to make himself ill. If he's had a shock he'd better see a doctor. Well, carry on, Merridew, and be sure you keep her warm and comfortable.

The damp is apt to come up through these brick floors. I'm thinking of having the whole place re-set with concrete, but it takes money, of course. I can't imagine,' he went on, as he led the way past the greenhouse towards a trim cottage set in its own square of kitchen-garden, 'what can have happened to have upset Plunkett. I hope it's nothing serious. He's getting elderly, of course, but he ought to be above believing in warnings. You wouldn't believe the extraordinary ideas these people get hold of. Fact is, I expect he's been round at the "Weary Traveller" and caught sight of somebody's washing hung out on the way home.'

'Not washing,' corrected Wimsey mechanically. He had a deductive turn of mind which exposed the folly of the suggestion even while irritably admitting that the matter was of no importance. 'It poured with rain last night, and, besides, it's Thursday. But Tuesday and Wednesday were fine, so the drying would have all been done then. No washing.'

'Well, well – something else then – a post, or old Mrs Giddens's white donkey. Plunkett does occasionally take a drop too much, I'm sorry to say, but he's a very good kennel-man, so one overlooks it. They're superstitious round about these parts, and they can tell some queer tales if once you get into their confidence. You'd be surprised how far off the main track we are as regards civilisation. Why, not here, but at Abbotts Bolton, fifteen miles off, it's as much as one's life's worth to shoot a hare. Witches, you know, and that sort of thing.'

'I shouldn't be a bit surprised. They'll still tell you about werewolves in some parts of Germany.'

'Yes, I dare say. Well, here we are.' Mr Frobisher-Pym

rapped loudly with his walking-stick on the door of the cottage and turned the handle without waiting for permission.

'You there, Mrs Plunkett? May we come in? Ah! good morning. Hope we're not disturbing you, but Merridew told me Plunkett was not so well. This is Lord Peter Wimsey – a very old friend of mine; that is to say, I'm a very old friend of *his*; ha, ha!'

'Good morning, sir; good morning, your lordship. I'm sure Plunkett will be very pleased to see you. Please step in. Plunkett, here's Mr Pym to see you.'

The elderly man who sat crouching over the fire turned a mournful face towards them, and half rose, touching his forehead.

'Well, now, Plunkett, what's the trouble?' enquired Mr Frobisher-Pym, with the hearty bedside manner adopted by country gentlefolk visiting their dependants. 'Sorry not to see you out and about. Touch of the old complaint, eh?'

'No, sir; no, sir. Thank you, sir. I'm well enough in myself. But I've had a warning, and I'm not long for this world.'

'Not long for this world? Oh, nonsense, Plunkett. You mustn't talk like that. A touch of indigestion, that's what you've got, I expect. Gives one the blues, I know. I'm sure I often feel like nothing on earth when I've got one of my bilious attacks. Try a dose of castor-oil, or a good old-fashioned blue pill and black draught. Nothing like it. Then you won't talk about warnings and dying.'

'No medicine won't do no good to *my* complaint, sir. Nobody as see what I've seed ever got the better of it. But as you and the gentleman are here, sir, I'm wondering if you'll do me a favour.'

'Of course, Plunkett, anything you like. What is it?'

'Why, just to draw up my will, sir. Old Parson, he used to do it. But I don't fancy this new young man, with his candles and bits of things. It don't seem as if he'd make it good and legal, sir, and I wouldn't like it if there was any dispute after I was gone. So as there ain't much time left me, I'd be grateful if you'd put it down clear for me in pen and ink that I wants my little bit all to go to Sarah here, and after her to Alf and Elsie, divided up equal.'

'Of course I'll do that for you, Plunkett, any time you like. But it's all nonsense to be talking about wills. Bless my soul, I shouldn't be surprised if you were to see us all underground.'

'No, sir. I've been a hale and hearty man, I'm not denying. But I've been called, sir, and I've got to go. It must come to all of us, I know that. But it's a fearful thing to see the death-coach come for one, and know that the dead are in it, that cannot rest in the grave.'

'Come now, Plunkett, you don't mean to tell me you believe in that old foolishness about the death-coach. I thought you were an educated man. What would Alf say if he heard you talking such nonsense?'

'Ah, sir, young people don't know everything, and there's many more things in God's creation than what you'll find in the printed books.'

'Oh, well,' said Mr Frobisher-Pym, finding this opening irresistible, 'we know there are more things in heaven and earth, Horatio, than are dreamt of in your philosophy. Quite so. But that doesn't apply nowadays,' he added contradictorily. 'There are no ghosts in the twentieth century. Just you think the matter out quietly, and you'll find you've made a mistake. There's probably some quite simple explanation. Dear me! I remember Mrs Frobisher-Pym waking up one night and having a terrible fright, because she thought somebody'd been and hanged himself on our bedroom door. Such a silly idea, because I was safe in bed beside her – snoring, *she* said, ha, ha! – and, if anybody was feeling like hanging himself, he wouldn't come into our bedroom to do it. Well, she clutched my arm in a great state of mind, and when I went to see what had alarmed her, what do you think it was? My trousers, which I'd hung up by the braces, with the socks still in the legs! My word! And didn't I get a wigging for not having put my things away tidy!'

Mr Frobisher-Pym laughed, and Mrs Plunkett said dutifully, 'There now!' Her husband shook his head.

'That may be, sir, but I see the death-coach last night with my own eyes. Just striking midnight it was, by the church clock, and I see it come up the lane by the old priory wall.'

'And what were you doing out of bed at midnight, eh?'

'Well, sir, I'd been round to my sister's, that's got her boy home on leaf off of his ship.'

'And you'd been drinking his health, I dare say, Plunkett.' Mr Frobisher-Pym wagged an admonitory forefinger.

'No, sir, I don't deny I'd had a glass or two of ale, but not to fuddle me. My wife can tell you I was sober enough when I got home.'

'That's right, sir. Plunkett hadn't taken too much last night, that I'll swear to.'

'Well, what was it you saw, Plunkett?'

'I see the death-coach, same as I'm telling you, sir. It come up the lane, all ghostly white, sir, and never making no more sound than the dead – which it were, sir.'

'A wagon or something going through to Lymptree or Herriotting.'

'No, sir – 'tweren't a wagon. I counted the horses – four white horses, and they went by with never a sound of hoof or bridle. And that weren't—'

'Four horses! Come, Plunkett, you must have been seeing double. There's nobody about here would be driving four horses, unless it was Mr Mortimer from Abbotts Bolton, and he wouldn't be taking his horseflesh out at midnight.'

'Four horses they was, sir. I see them plain. And it weren't Mr Mortimer, neither, for he drives a drag, and this were a big, heavy coach, with no lights on it, but shinin' all of itself, with a colour like moonshine.'

'Oh, nonsense, man! You couldn't see the moon last night. It was pitch-dark.'

'No, sir, but the coach shone all moony-like, all the same.'

'And no lights? I wonder what the police would say to that.'

'No mortal police could stop that coach,' said Plunkett contemptuously, 'nor no mortal man could abide the sight on it. I tell you, sir, that ain't the worst of it. The horses—'

'Was it going slowly?'

'No, sir. It were going at a gallop, only the hoofs didn't touch the ground. There weren't no sound, and I see the black road and the white hoofs half a foot off of it. And the horses had no heads.'

'No heads?'

'No, sir.'

Mr Frobisher-Pym laughed.

'Come, come, Plunkett, you don't expect us to swallow that. No heads? How could even a ghost drive horses with no heads? How about the reins, eh?'

'You may laugh, sir, but we know that with God all things are possible. Four white horses they was. I see them clearly, but there was neither head nor neck beyond the collar, sir. I see the reins, shining like silver, and they ran up to the rings of the hames, and they didn't go no further. If I was to drop down dead this minute, sir, that's what I see.'

'Was there a driver to this wonderful turn-out?'

'Yes, sir, there was a driver.'

'Headless too, I suppose?'

'Yes, sir, headless too. At least, I couldn't see nothing of him beyond his coat, which had them old-fashioned capes at the shoulders.'

'Well, I must say, Plunkett, you're very circumstantial. How far off was this – er – apparition when you saw it?'

'I was passing by the War Memorial, sir, when I see it come up the lane. It wouldn't be above twenty or thirty yards from where I stood. It went by at a gallop, and turned off to the left round the churchyard wall.'

'Well, well, it sounds odd, certainly, but it was a dark night, and at that distance your eyes may have deceived you. Now, if you'll take my advice you'll think no more about it.'

'Ah, sir, it's all very well saying that, but everybody knows the man who sees the death-coach of the Burdocks is doomed to die within the week. There's no use rebelling against it, sir; it is so. And if you'll be so good as to oblige

me over that matter of a will, I'd die happier for knowing as
Sarah and the children was sure of their bit of money.'

Mr Frobisher-Pym obliged over the will, though much
against the grain, exhorting and scolding as he wrote.
Wimsey added his own signature as one of the witnesses,
and contributed his own bit of comfort.

'I shouldn't worry too much about the coach, if I were
you,' he said. 'Depend upon it, if it's the Burdock coach it'll
just have come for the soul of the old squire. It couldn't be
expected to go to New York for him, don't you see? It's just
gettin' ready for the funeral tomorrow.'

'That's likely enough,' agreed Plunkett. 'Often and often
it's been seen in these parts when one of the Burdocks was
taken. But it's terrible unlucky to see it.'

The thought of the funeral seemed, however, to cheer him
a little. The visitors again begged him not to think about it,
and took their departure.

'Isn't it wonderful,' said Mr Frobisher-Pym, 'what imagination will do with these people? And they're obstinate. You
could argue with them till you were black in the face.'

'Yes. I say, let's go down to the church and have a look at
the place. I'd like to know how much he could really have
seen from where he was standing.'

The parish church of Little Doddering stands, like so
many country churches, at some distance from the houses.
The main road from Herriotting, Abbotts Bolton and
Frimpton runs past the west gate of the churchyard – a wide
God's acre, crowded with ancient stones. On the south side
is a narrow and gloomy lane, heavily overhung with old
elm-trees, dividing the church from the still more ancient

ruins of Doddering Priory. On the main road, a little beyond the point where Old Priory Lane enters, stands the War Memorial, and from here the road runs straight on into Little Doddering. Round the remaining two sides of the church-yard winds another lane, known to the village simply as the Back Lane. This branches out from the Herriotting road about a hundred yards north of the church, connects with the far end of Priory Lane, and thence proceeds deviously to Shootering Underwood, Hamsey, Thripsey and Wyck.

'Whatever it was Plunkett thinks he saw,' said Mr Frobisher-Pym, 'it must have come from Shootering. The Back Lane only leads round by some fields and a cottage or two, and it stands to reason anybody coming from Frimpton would have taken the main road, going and coming. The lane is in a very bad state with all this rain. I'm afraid even your detective ability, my dear Wimsey, would not avail to find wheel-marks on this modern tarmac.'

'Hardly,' said Wimsey, 'especially in the case of a ghostly chariot which gets along without touching the ground. But your reasoning seems perfectly sound, sir.'

'It was probably a couple of belated wagons going to market,' pursued Mr Frobisher-Pym, 'and the rest of it is superstition and, I am afraid, the local beer. Plunkett couldn't have seen all those details about drivers and hames and so on at this distance. And, if it was making no noise, how did he come to notice it at all, since he'd got past the turn and was walking in the other direction? Depend upon it, he heard the wheels and imagined the rest.'

'Probably,' said Wimsey.

'Of course,' went on his host, 'if the wagons really were

going about without lights, it ought to be looked into. It is a very dangerous thing, with all these motor vehicles about, and I've had to speak severely about it before now. I fined a man only the other day for the very same thing. Do you care to see the church while we're here?'

Knowing that in country places it is always considered proper to see the church, Lord Peter expressed his eagerness to do so.

'It's always open nowadays,' said the magistrate, leading the way to the west entrance. 'The vicar has an idea that churches should be always open for private prayer. He comes from a town living, of course. Round about here the people are always out on the land, and you can't expect them to come into church in their working clothes and muddy boots. They wouldn't think it respectful, and they've other things to do. Besides, I said to him, consider the opportunity it gives for undesirable conduct. But he's a young man, and he'll have to learn by experience.'

He pushed the door open. A curious, stuffy waft of stale incense, damp and stoves rushed out at them as they entered – a kind of concentrated extract of Church of England. The two altars, bright with flowers and gilding, and showing as garish splashes among the heavy shadows and oppressive architecture of the little Norman building, sounded the same note of contradiction; it was the warm and human that seemed exotic and unfamiliar; the cold and unwelcoming that seemed native to the place and people.

'This Lady-chapel, as Hancock calls it, in the south aisle, is new, of course,' said Mr Frobisher-Pym. 'It aroused a good deal of opposition, but the Bishop is lenient with the

High Church party – too lenient, some people think – but, after all, what does it matter? I'm sure I can say my prayers just as well with two communion-tables as with one. And, I will say for Hancock, he is very good with the young men and the girls. In these days of motor-cycles, it's something to get them interested in religion at all. Those trestles in the chapel are for old Burdock's coffin, I suppose. Ah! Here is the vicar.'

A thin man in a cassock emerged from a door beside the high altar and came down towards them, carrying a tall, oaken candlestick in his hand. He greeted them with a slightly professional smile of welcome. Wimsey diagnosed him promptly as earnest, nervous, and not highly intellectual.

'The candlesticks have only just come,' he observed after the usual introductions had been made. 'I was afraid they would not be here in time. However, all is now well.'

He set the candlestick beside the coffin-trestles, and proceeded to decorate its brass spike with a long candle of unbleached wax, which he took from a parcel in a neighbouring pew.

Mr Frobisher-Pym said nothing. Wimsey felt it incumbent on him to express his interest, and did so.

'It is very gratifying,' said Mr Hancock, thus encouraged, 'to see the people beginning to take a real interest in their church. I have really had very little difficulty in finding watchers for tonight. We are having eight watchers, two by two, from 10 o'clock this evening – till which time I shall be myself on duty – till six in the morning, when I come in to say Mass. The men will carry on till 2 o'clock, then my wife and daughter will relieve them, and Mr Hubbard and young Rawlinson have kindly consented to take the hours from four till six.'

'What Rawlinson is that?' demanded Mr Frobisher-Pym.

'Mr Graham's clerk from Herriotting. It is true he is not a member of the parish, but he was born here, and was good enough to wish to take his turn in watching. He is coming over on his motor-cycle. After all, Mr Graham has had charge of Burdock's family affairs for very many years, and no doubt they wished to show their respect in some way.'

'Well, I only hope he'll be awake enough to do his work in the morning, after gadding about all night,' said Mr Frobisher-Pym gruffly. 'As for Hubbard, that's his own look-out, though I must say it seems an odd occupation for a publican. Still, if he's pleased, and you're pleased, there's no more to be said about it.'

'You've got a very beautiful old church here, Mr Hancock,' said Wimsey, seeing that controversy seemed imminent.

'Very beautiful indeed,' said the vicar. 'Have you noticed that apse? It is rare for a village church to possess such a perfect Norman apse. Perhaps you would like to come and look at it.' He genuflected as they passed a hanging lamp which burned before a niche. 'You see, we are permitted Reservation. The Bishop—' He prattled cheerfully as they wandered up the chancel, digressing from time to time to draw attention to the handsome miserere seats ('Of course, this was the original Priory Church'), and a beautifully carved piscina and aumbry ('It is rare to find them so well preserved'). Wimsey assisted him to carry down the remaining candlesticks from the vestry, and, when these had been put in position, joined Mr Frobisher-Pym at the door.

*

'I think you said you were dining with the Lumsdens tonight,' said the magistrate, as they sat smoking after lunch. 'How are you going? Will you have the car?'

'I'd rather you'd lend me one of the saddle-horses,' said Wimsey. 'I get few opportunities of riding in town.'

'Certainly, my dear boy, certainly. Only I'm afraid you'll have rather a wet ride. Take Polly Flinders; it will do her good to get some exercise. You are quite sure you would prefer it? Have you got your kit with you?'

'Yes – I brought an old pair of bags down with me, and, with this raincoat, I shan't come to any harm. They won't expect me to dress. How far is it to Frimpton, by the way?'

'Nine miles by the main road, and tarmac all the way, I'm afraid, but there's a good wide piece of grass each side. And, of course, you can cut off a mile or so by going across the common. What time will you want to start?'

'Oh, about seven o'clock, I should think. And, I say, sir – will Mrs Frobisher-Pym think it very rude if I'm rather late back? Old Lumsden and I went through the War together, and if we get yarning over old times we may go on into the small hours. I don't want to feel I'm treating your house like a hotel, but—'

'Of course not, of course not! That's absolutely all right. My wife won't mind in the very least. We want you to enjoy your visit and do exactly what you like. I'll give you the key, and I'll remember not to put the chain up. Perhaps you wouldn't mind doing that yourself when you come in?'

'Rather not. And how about the mare?'

'I'll tell Merridew to look out for you; he sleeps over the

stables. I only wish it were going to be a better night for you. I'm afraid the glass is going back. Yes. Dear, dear! It's a bad look-out for tomorrow. By the way, you'll probably pass the funeral procession at the church. It should be along by about then, if the train is punctual.'

The train, presumably, was punctual, for as Lord Peter cantered up to the west gate of the church he saw a hearse of great funereal pomp drawn up before it, surrounded by a little crowd of people. Two mourning coaches were in attend-ance; the driver of the second seemed to be having some difficulty with the horses, and Wimsey rightly inferred that this was the pair which had been borrowed from Mr Mor-timer. Restraining Polly Flinders as best he might, he sidled into a respectful position on the edge of the crowd, and watched the coffin taken from the hearse and carried through the gate, where it was met by Mr Hancock, in full pontifi-cals, attended by a thurifer and two torch-bearers. The effect was a little marred by the rain, which had extinguished the candles, but the village seemed to look upon it as an excellent show nevertheless. A massive man, dressed with great cor-rectness in a black frock coat and tall hat, and accompanied by a woman in handsome mourning and furs, was sympa-thetically commented on. This was Haviland Burdock of silk-stocking fame, the younger son of the deceased. A vast number of white wreaths were then handed out, and greeted with murmurs of admiration and approval. The choir struck up a hymn, rather raggedly, and the procession filed away into the church. Polly Flinders shook her head vigorously, and Wimsey, taking this as a signal to be gone, replaced his hat and ambled gently away towards Frimpton.

He followed the main road for about four miles, winding up through finely wooded country to the edge of Frimpton Common. Here the road made a wide sweep, skirting the common and curving gently down into Frimpton village. Wimsey hesitated for a moment, considering that it was growing dark and that both the way and the animal he rode were strange to him. There seemed, however, to be a well-defined bridle-path across the common, and eventually he decided to take it. Polly Flinders seemed to know it well enough, and cantered along without hesitation. A ride of about a mile and a half brought them without adventure into the main road again. Here a fork in the road presented itself confusingly; an electric torch, however, and a signpost solved the problem; after which ten minutes' ride brought the traveller to his goal.

Major Lumsden was a large, cheerful man – none the less cheerful for having lost a leg in the War. He had a large, cheerful wife, a large, cheerful house, and a large, cheerful family. Wimsey soon found himself seated before a fire as large and cheerful as the rest of the establishment, exchanging gossip with his hosts over a whisky-and-soda. He described the Burdock funeral with irreverent gusto, and went on to tell the story of the phantom coach. Major Lumsden laughed.

'It's a quaint part of the country,' he said. 'The policeman is just as bad as the rest of them. Do you remember, dear, the time I had to go out and lay a ghost, down at Pogson's farm?'

'I do, indeed,' said his wife emphatically. 'The maids had a wonderful time. Trivett – that's our local constable – came rushing in here and fainted in the kitchen, and they all sat round howling and sustaining him with our best brandy, while Dan went down and investigated.'

'Did you find the ghost?'

'Well, not the ghost, exactly, but we found a pair of boots and half a pork-pie in the empty house, so we put it all down to a tramp. Still, I must say odd things do happen about here. There were those fires on the common last year. They were never explained.'

'Gipsies, Dan.'

'Maybe; but nobody ever saw them, and the fires would start in the most unexpected way, sometimes in the pouring rain; and, before you could get near one, it would be out, and only a sodden wet black mark left behind it. And there's another bit of the common that animals don't like – near what they call the Dead Man's Post. My dogs won't go near it. Funny brutes. I've never seen anything there, but even in broad daylight they don't seem to fancy it. The common's not got a good reputation. It used to be a great place for highwaymen.'

'Is the Burdock coach anything to do with highwaymen?'

'No. I fancy it was some rakehelly dead-and-gone Burdock. Belonged to the Hell-fire Club or something. The usual sort of story. All the people round here believe in it, of course. It's rather a good thing. Keeps the servants indoors at night. Well, let's go and have some grub, shall we?'

'Do you remember,' said Major Lumsden, 'that damned old mill, and the three elms by the pigsty?'

'Good Lord, yes! You very obligingly blew them out of the landscape for us, I remember. They made us a damned sight too conspicuous.'

'We rather missed them when they were gone.'

'Thank heaven you didn't miss them when they were there. I'll tell you what you did miss, though.'

'What's that?'

'The old sow.'

'By Jove, yes. Do you remember old Piper fetching her in?'

'I'll say I do. That reminds me. You knew Bunthorne ...'

'I'll say good night,' said Mrs Lumsden, 'and leave you people to it.'

'Do you remember,' said Lord Peter Wimsey, 'that awkward moment when Popham went off his rocker?'

'No. I'd been sent back with a batch of prisoners. I heard about it though. I never knew what became of him.'

'I got him sent home. He's married now and living in Lincolnshire.'

'Is he? Well, he couldn't help himself, I suppose. He was only a kid. What's happened to Philpotts?'

'Oh, Philpotts ...'

'Where's your glass, old man?'

'Oh, rot, old man. The night is still young ...'

'Really? Well, but look here, why not stay the night? My wife will be delighted. I can fix you up in no time.'

'No, thanks most awfully. I must be rolling off home. I said I'd be back; and I'm booked to put the chain on the door.'

'As you like, of course, but it's still raining. Not a good night for a ride on an open horse.'

'I'll bring a saloon next time. We shan't hurt. Rain's good for the complexion – makes the roses grow. Don't wake your man up. I can saddle her myself.'

'My dear man, it's no trouble.'

'No, really, old man.'

'Well, I'll come along and lend you a hand.'

A gust of rain and wind blew in through the hall door as they struggled out into the night. It was past one in the morning and pitch-dark. Major Lumsden again pressed Wimsey to stay.

'No, thanks, really. The old lady's feelings might be hurt. It's not so bad, really – wet, but not cold. Come up, Polly, stand over, old lady.'

He put the saddle on and girthed it, while Lumsden held the lantern. The mare, fed and rested, came delicately dancing out of the warm loose-box, head well stretched forward, and nostrils snuffing at the rain.

'Well, so long, old lad. Come and look us up again. It's been great.'

'Rather! By Jove, yes. Best respects to madame. Is the gate open?'

'Yes.'

'Well, cheerio!'

'Cheerio!'

Polly Flinders, with her nose turned homewards, settled down to make short work of the nine miles of high-road. Once outside the gates, the night seemed lighter, though the rain poured heavily. Somewhere buried behind the thronging clouds there was a moon, which now and again showed as a pale stain on the sky, a paler reflection on the black road. Wimsey, with a mind full of memories and a skin full of whisky, hummed to himself as he rode.

As he passed the fork, he hesitated for a moment. Should

he take the path over the common or stick to the road? On consideration, he decided to give the common a miss – not because of its sinister reputation, but because of ruts and rabbit-holes. He shook the reins, bestowed a word of encouragement on his mount, and continued by the road, having the common on his right hand, and, on the left, fields bounded by high hedges, which gave some shelter from the driving rain.

He had topped the rise, and passed the spot where the bridle-path again joined the high-road, when a slight start and stumble drew his attention unpleasantly to Polly Flinders.

'Hold up, mare,' he said disapprovingly.

Polly shook her head, moved forward, tried to pick up her easy pace again. 'Hullo!' said Wimsey, alarmed. He pulled her to a standstill.

'Lame in the near fore,' he said, dismounting. 'If you've been and gone and strained anything, my girl, four miles from home, Father *will* be pleased.' It occurred to him for the first time how curiously lonely the road was. He had not seen a single car. They might have been in the wilds of Africa.

He ran an exploratory hand down the near foreleg. The mare stood quietly enough, without shrinking or wincing. Wimsey was puzzled.

'If these had been the good old days,' he said, 'I'd have thought she'd picked up a stone. But what—'

He lifted the mare's foot, and explored it carefully with fingers and pocket-torch. His diagnosis had been right, after all. A steel nut, evidently dropped from a passing car, had wedged itself firmly between the shoe and the frog. He grunted and felt for his knife. Happily, it was one of that excellent old-fashioned kind which includes, besides blades and corkscrews, an ingenious apparatus for removing foreign bodies from horses' feet.

The mare nuzzled him gently as he stooped over his task. It was a little awkward getting to work; he had to wedge the torch under his arm, so as to leave one hand free for the tool and the other to hold the hoof. He was swearing gently at these difficulties when, happening to glance down the road ahead, he fancied he caught the gleam of something moving. It was not easy to see, for at this point the tall trees stood up on both sides of the road, which dipped abruptly from the edge of the common. It was not a car; the light was too faint. A wagon, probably, with a dim lantern. Yet it seemed to move fast. He puzzled for a moment, then bent to work again.

The nut resisted his efforts, and the mare, touched in a tender spot, pulled away, trying to get her foot down. He soothed her with his voice and patted her neck. The torch slipped from his arm. He cursed it impatiently, set down the hoof, and picked up the torch from the edge of the grass, into which it had rolled. As he straightened himself again, he looked along the road and saw.

Up from under the dripping dark of the trees it came, shining with a thin, moony radiance. There was no clatter of hoofs, no rumble of wheels, no ringing of bit or bridle. He saw the white, sleek, shining shoulders with the collar that lay on each, like a faint fiery ring, enclosing nothing. He saw the gleaming reins, their cut ends slipping back and forward unsupported through the ring of the hames. The feet, that never touched earth, ran swiftly – four times four noiseless hoofs, bearing the pale bodies by like smoke. The driver leaned forward, brandishing his whip. He was faceless and headless, but his whole attitude bespoke desperate haste. The coach was barely visible through the driving rain, but Wimsey saw the dimly spinning wheels and a faint whiteness, still and stiff, at the window. It went past at a gallop – headless driver and headless horse and silent coach. Its passing left a stir, a sound that was less a sound than a vibration – and the wind roared suddenly after it, with a great sheet of water blown up out of the south.

'Good God!' said Wimsey. And then: 'How many whiskies did we have?'

He turned and looked back along the road, straining his eyes. Then suddenly he remembered the mare, and, without troubling further about the torch, picked up her foot and went to work by touch. The nut gave no more trouble, but dropped out into his hand almost immediately. Polly Flinders sighed gratefully and blew into his ear.

Wimsey led her forward a few steps. She put her feet down firmly and strongly. The nut, removed without delay, had left no tenderness. Wimsey mounted, let her go – then pulled her head round suddenly.

'I'm going to see,' he said resolutely. 'Come up, mare! We won't let any headless horses get the better of *us*. Perfectly indecent, goin' about without heads. Get on, old lady. Over the common with you. We'll catch 'em at the cross-roads.'

Without the slightest consideration for his host or his host's property, he put the mare to the bridle-path again, and urged her into a gallop.

At first he thought he could make out a pale, fluttering

whiteness, moving away ahead of him on the road. Presently, as high-road and bridle-path diverged, he lost it altogether. But he knew there was no side-road. Bar any accident to his mount, he was bound to catch it before it came to the fork. Polly Flinders, answering easily to the touch of his heel, skimmed over the rough track with the indifference born of familiarity. In less than ten minutes her feet rang out again on the tarmac. He pulled her up, faced round in the direction of Little Doddering, and stared down the road. He could see nothing yet. Either he was well ahead of the coach, or it had already passed at unbelievable speed, or else—

He waited. Nothing. The violent rain had ceased, and the moon was struggling out again. The road appeared completely deserted. He glanced over his shoulder. A small beam of light near the ground moved, turned, flashed green, and red, and white again, and came towards him. Presently he made out that it was a policeman wheeling a bicycle.

'A bad night, sir,' said the man civilly, but with a faint note of enquiry in his voice.

'Rotten,' said Wimsey.

'Just had to mend a puncture, to make it all the pleasanter,' added the policeman.

Wimsey expressed sympathy. 'Have you been here long?' he added.

'Best part o' twenty minutes.'

'Did you see anything pass along this way from Little Doddering?'

'Ain't been nothing along while I've been here. What sort of thing did you mean, sir?'

'I thought I saw—' Wimsey hesitated. He did not care

about the idea of making a fool of himself. 'A carriage with four horses,' he said hesitatingly. 'It passed me on this road not a quarter of an hour ago – down at the other end of the common. I – I came back to see. It seemed unusual—' He became aware that his story sounded very lame.

The policeman spoke rather sharply and rapidly.

'There ain't been nothing past here.'

'You're sure?'

'Yes, sir; and, if you don't mind me sayin' so, you'd best be getting home. It's a lonesome bit o' road.'

'Yes, isn't it?' said Wimsey. 'Well, good night, sergeant.'

He turned the mare's head back along the Little Doddering road, going very quietly. He saw nothing, heard nothing, and passed nothing. The night was brighter now, and, as he rode back, he verified the entire absence of side-roads. Whatever the thing was which he had seen, it had vanished somewhere along the edge of the common; it had not gone by the main road, nor by any other.

Wimsey came down rather late for breakfast in the morning, to find his hosts in a state of some excitement.

'The most extraordinary thing has happened,' said Mrs Frobisher-Pym.

'Outrageous!' added her husband. 'I warned Hancock – he can't say I didn't warn him. Still, however much one may disapprove of his goings-on, there is no excuse whatever for such abominable conduct. Once let me get hold of the beggars, whoever they are—'

'What's up?' said Wimsey, helping himself to broiled kidneys at the sideboard.

'A most scandalous thing,' said Mrs Frobisher-Pym. 'The vicar came up to Tom at once – I hope we didn't disturb you, by the way, with all the excitement. It appears that when Mr Hancock got to the church this morning at 6 o'clock to take the early service—'

'No, no, my dear, you've got it wrong. Let *me* tell it. When Joe Grinch – that's the sexton, you know, and he has to get there first to ring the bell – when he arrived, he found the south door wide open and nobody in the chapel, where they should have been, beside the coffin. He was very much perplexed, of course, but he supposed that Hubbard and young Rawlinson had got sick of it and gone off home. So he went on to the vestry to get the vestments and things ready, and to his amazement he heard women's voices, calling out to him from inside. He was so astonished, didn't know where he was, but he went on and unlocked the door—'

'With his own key?' put in Wimsey.

'The key was in the door. As a rule it's kept hanging up on a nail under a curtain near the organ, but it was in the lock – where it ought not to have been. And inside the vestry he found Mrs Hancock and her daughter, nearly dead with fright and annoyance.'

'Great Scott!'

'Yes, indeed. They had a most extraordinary story to tell. They'd taken over at 2 o'clock from the other pair of watchers, and had knelt down by the coffin in the Lady-chapel, according to plan, to say the proper sort of prayers, whatever they are. They'd been there, to the best of their calculation, about ten minutes, when they heard a noise up by the high altar, as though somebody was creeping stealthily about. Miss

Hancock is a very plucky girl, and she got up and walked up the aisle in the dark, with Mrs Hancock following on behind because, as she said, she didn't want to be left alone. When they'd got as far as the rood-screen, Miss Hancock called out aloud, "Who's there?" At that they heard a sort of rustling sound, and a noise like something being knocked over. Miss Hancock most courageously snatched up one of the churchwarden's staffs, which was clipped on to the choir-stalls, and ran forward, thinking, she says, that somebody was trying to steal the ornaments off the altar. There's a very fine fifteenth-century cross—'

'Never mind the cross, Tom. That hasn't been taken, at any rate.'

'No, it hasn't, but she thought it might be. Anyhow, just as she got up to the sanctuary steps, with Mrs Hancock coming close after her and begging her to be careful, somebody seemed to rush out of the choir-stalls, and caught her by the arms and frog's-marched her – that's her expression – into the vestry. And before she could get breath even to shriek, Mrs Hancock was pushed in beside her, and the door locked on them.'

'By Jove! You do have exciting times in your village.'

'Well,' said Mr Frobisher-Pym, 'of course they were dreadfully frightened, because they didn't know but what these wretches would come back and murder them, and, in any case, they thought the church was being robbed. But the vestry windows are very narrow and barred, and they couldn't do anything except wait. They tried to listen, but they couldn't hear much. Their only hope was that the four o'clock watchers might come early and catch the thieves at work. But they waited and they waited, and they heard four strike, and five, and nobody came.'

'What had happened to what's-his-name and Rawlinson then?'

'They couldn't make out, and nor could Grinch. However, they had a good look round the church, and nothing seemed to be taken or disturbed in any way. Just then the vicar came along, and they told him all about it. He was very much shocked, naturally, and his first thought – when he found the ornaments were safe and the poor-box all right – was that some Kensitite people had been stealing the wafers from the what d'you call it.'

'The tabernacle,' suggested Wimsey.

'Yes, that's his name for it. That worried him very much, and he unlocked it and had a look, but the wafers were all there all right, and, as there's only one key, and that was on his own watch-chain, it wasn't a case of anyone substituting unconsecrated wafers for consecrated ones, or any practical joke of that kind. So he sent Mrs and Miss Hancock home, and had a look round the church outside, and the first thing he saw, lying in the bushes near the south door, was young Rawlinson's motor-cycle.'

'Oho!'

'So his next idea was to hunt for Rawlinson and Hubbard. However, he didn't have to look far. He'd got round the church as far as the furnace-house on the north side, when he heard a terrific hullabaloo going on, and people shouting and thumping on the door. So he called Grinch, and they looked in through the little window, and there, if you please, were Hubbard and young Rawlinson, bawling and going on and using the most shocking language. It seems they were set on in exactly the same way, only before they got inside the church. Rawlinson had been passing the evening with Hubbard, I understand, and they had a bit of a sleep downstairs in the back bar, to avoid disturbing the house early – or so they say, though I dare say if the truth was known they were having drinks; and if that's Hancock's idea of a suitable preparation for going to church and saying prayers, all I can say is, it isn't mine. Anyway, they started off just before four, Hubbard going down on the carrier of Rawlinson's bicycle. They had to get off at the south gate, which was pushed to, and while Rawlinson was wheeling the machine up the path two or three men – they couldn't see exactly – jumped out from the trees. There was a bit of a scuffle, but what with the bicycle, and its being so unexpected, they couldn't put up a very good fight, and the men dropped blankets over their heads, or something. I don't know all the details. At any rate, they were bundled into the furnace-house and left there. They may be there still, for all I know, if they haven't found the key. There should be a spare key, but I don't know what's become of it. They sent up for it this morning, but I haven't seen it about for a long time.'

'It wasn't left in the lock this time, then?'

'No, it wasn't. They've had to send for the locksmith. I'm going down now to see what's to be done about it. Like to come, if you're ready?'

Wimsey said he would. Anything in the nature of a problem always fascinated him.

'You were back pretty late, by the way,' said Mr Frobisher-Pym jovially, as they left the house. 'Yarning over old times, I suppose.'

'We were, indeed,' said Wimsey.

'Hope the old girl carried you all right. Lonely bit of road, isn't it? I don't suppose you saw anybody worse than yourself, as the saying goes?'

'Only a policeman,' said Wimsey untruthfully. He had not yet quite decided about the phantom coach. No doubt Plunkett would be relieved to know that he was not the only person to whom the 'warning' had come. But, then, had it really been the phantom coach, or merely a delusion, begotten by whisky upon reminiscence? Wimsey, in the cold light of day, was none too certain.

On arriving at the church, the magistrate and his guest found quite a little crowd collected, conspicuous among whom were the vicar, in cassock and biretta, gesticulating freely, and the local policeman, his tunic buttoned awry and his dignity much impaired by the small fry of the village, who clustered round his legs. He had just finished taking down the statements of the two men who had been released from the stoke-hole. The younger of these, a fresh-faced, impudent-looking fellow of twenty-five or so, was in the act of starting up his motor-cycle. He greeted Mr Frobisher-Pym pleasantly. 'Afraid they've made us look a bit small, sir. You'll excuse me, won't you? I'll have to be getting back to Herriotting. Mr Graham won't be any too pleased if I'm late for the office. I think some of the bright lads have been having a joke with us.' He grinned as he pushed the throttle-lever over and departed in a smother of unnecessary smoke that made Mr Frobisher-Pym sneeze. His fellow-victim, a large, fat man, who looked the sporting publican that he was, grinned shamefacedly at the magistrate.

'Well, Hubbard,' said the latter, 'I hope you've enjoyed your experience. I must say I'm surprised at a man of your size letting himself be shut up in a coal-hole like a naughty urchin.'

'Yes, sir, I was surprised myself at the time,' retorted the publican, good-humouredly enough. 'When that there blanket came down on my head, I was the most surprised man in this here country. I gave 'em a hack or two on the shins, though, to remember me by,' he added, with a reminiscent chuckle.

'How many of them were there?' asked Wimsey.

'Three or four, I should say, sir. But not 'avin' seen 'em, I can only tell from 'earin' 'em talk. There was two laid 'old of me, I'm pretty sure, and young Rawlinson thinks there was only one 'ad 'old of 'im, but 'e was a wonderful strong 'un.'

'We must leave no stone unturned to find out who these people were,' said the vicar excitedly. 'Ah, Mr Frobisher-Pym, come and see what they have done in the church. It is as I thought – an anti-Catholic protest. We must be most thankful that they have done no more than they have.'

He led the way in. Someone had lit two or three hanging lamps in the gloomy little chancel. By their light Wimsey was able to see that the neck of the eagle lectern was decorated with an enormous red-white-and-blue bow, and bore a large placard – obviously pinched from the local newspaper offices – 'Vatican Bans Immodest Dress'. In each of the choir-stalls a teddy-bear sat, lumpishly amiable, apparently absorbed in reading the choir-books upside-down, while on the ledge before them copies of the *Pink 'Un* were obtrusively displayed. In the pulpit, a waggish hand had set up a pantomime ass's head, elegantly arrayed in a nightgown, and crowned with a handsome nimbus, cut from gold paper.

'Disgraceful, isn't it?' said the vicar.

'Well, Hancock,' replied Mr Frobisher-Pym, 'I must say I think you have brought it upon yourself – though I quite agree, of course, that this sort of thing cannot possibly be allowed, and the offenders must be discovered and severely punished. But you must see that many of your practices appear to these people to be papistical nonsense at best, and while that is no excuse ...'

His reprimanding voice barked on.

'... what I really can only look upon as this sacrilegious business with old Burdock – a man whose life ...'

The policeman had by this time shoved away the attendant villagers and was standing beside Lord Peter at the entrance of the rood-screen.

'Was that you was out on the road this morning, sir? Ah! I thought I reckernised your voice. Did you get home all right, sir? Didn't meet nothing?'

There seemed to be a shade more than idle questioning in the tone of his voice. Wimsey turned quickly.

'No, I met nothing – more. Who is it drives a coach with four white horses about this village of a night, sergeant?'

'Not sergeant, sir – I ain't due for promotion yet awhile. Well, sir, as to white horses, I don't altogether like to say. Mr Mortimer over at Abbotts Bolton has some nice greys, and he's the biggest horse-breeder about these parts – but, well, there, sir, he wouldn't be driving out in all that rain, sir, would he?'

'It doesn't seem a sensible thing to do, certainly.'

'No, sir. And' – the constable leaned close to Wimsey and spoke into his ear – 'and Mr Mortimer is a man that's got a head on his shoulders – *and, what's more, so have his horses.*'

'Why,' said Wimsey, a little startled by the aptness of this remark, 'did you ever know a horse that hadn't?'

'No, sir,' said the policeman, with emphasis, 'I never knew no *livin'* horse that hadn't. But that's neether here nor there, as the sayin' goes. But as to this church business, that's just a bit of a lark got up among the boys, that's what that is. They don't mean no harm, you know, sir; they likes to be up to their tricks. It's all very well for the vicar to talk, sir, but this ain't no Kensitites nor anythink of that, as you can see with half an eye. Just a bit of fun, that's all it is.'

'I'd come to the same conclusion myself,' said Wimsey, interested, 'but I'd rather like to know what makes you think so.'

'Lord bless you, sir, ain't it plain as the nose on your face? If it had a-bin these Kensitites, wouldn't they have gone for the crosses and the images and the lights and – that there?' He extended a horny finger in the direction of the tabernacle. 'No, sir, these lads what did this ain't laid a finger on the things what you might call sacred images – and they ain't done no harm neether to the communion-table. So I says as it ain't a case of con*trov*versy, but more a bit of fun, like. And they've treated Mr Burdock's corpse respectful, sir, you see, too. That shows they wasn't meaning anything wrong at heart, don't you see?'

'I agree absolutely,' said Wimsey. 'In fact, they've taken particular care not to touch anything that a churchman holds really sacred. How long have you been on this job, officer?'

'Three years, sir, come February.'

'Ever had any idea of going to town or taking up the detective side of the business?'

'Well, sir – I have – but it isn't just ask and have, as you might say.'

Wimsey took a card from his note-case.

'If you ever think seriously about it,' he said, 'give this card to Chief Inspector Parker, and have a chat with him. Tell him I think you haven't got opportunities enough down here. He's a great friend of mine, and he'll give you a good chance, I know.'

'I've heard of you, my lord,' said the constable, gratified, 'and I'm sure it's very kind of your lordship. Well, I suppose I'd best be getting along now. You leave it to me, Mr Frobisher-Pym, sir; we'll soon get at the bottom of this here.'

'I hope you do,' said the magistrate. 'Meanwhile, Mr Hancock, I trust you will realise the inadvisability of leaving the church doors open at night. Well, come along, Wimsey; we'll leave them to get the church straight for the funeral. What have you found there?'

'Nothing,' said Wimsey, who had been peering at the floor of the Lady-chapel. 'I was afraid you'd got the worm in here, but I see it's only sawdust.' He dusted his fingers as he spoke, and followed Mr Frobisher-Pym out of the building.

When you are staying in a village, you are expected to take part in the interests and amusements of the community. Accordingly, Lord Peter duly attended the funeral of Squire Burdock, and beheld the coffin safely committed to the ground, in a drizzle, certainly, but not without the attendance of a large and reverent congregation. After this ceremony, he was formally introduced to Mr and Mrs Haviland Burdock, and was able to confirm his previous impression that the lady was well, not to say too well, dressed, as might be expected from one whose wardrobe was based upon silk stockings. She was a handsome woman, in a large, bold style, and the hand that clasped Wimsey's was quite painfully encrusted with diamonds. Haviland was disposed to be friendly – and, indeed, silk manufacturers have no reason to be otherwise to rich men of noble birth. He seemed to be aware of Wimsey's reputation as an antiquarian and book-collector, and extended a hearty invitation to him to come and see the old house.

'My brother Martin is still abroad,' he said, 'but I'm sure he would be delighted to have you come and look at the place. I'm told there are some very fine old books in the library. We shall be staying here till Monday – if Mrs Hancock will be good enough to have us. Suppose you come along tomorrow afternoon.'

Wimsey said he would be delighted.

Mrs Hancock interposed and said, wouldn't Lord Peter come to tea at the vicarage first.

Wimsey said it was very good of her.

'Then that's settled,' said Mrs Burdock. 'You and Mr Pym come to tea, and then we'll all go over the house together. I've hardly seen it myself yet.'

'It's very well worth seeing,' said Mr Frobisher-Pym. 'Fine old place, but takes some money to keep up. Has nothing been seen of the will yet, Mr Burdock?'

'Nothing whatever,' said Haviland. 'It's curious, because

Mr Graham – the solicitor, you know, Lord Peter – certainly drew one up, just after poor Martin's unfortunate difference with our father. He remembers it perfectly.'

'Can't he remember what's in it?'

'He could, of course, but he doesn't think it etiquette to say. He's one of the crusted old type. Poor Martin always called him an old scoundrel – but then, of course, he never approved of Martin, so Martin was not altogether unprejudiced. Besides, as Mr Graham says, all that was some years ago, and it's quite possible that the governor destroyed the will later, or made a new one in America.'

'"Poor Martin" doesn't seem to have been popular hereabouts,' said Wimsey to Mr Frobisher-Pym, as they parted from the Burdocks and turned homewards.

'N-no,' said the magistrate. 'Not with Graham, anyway. Personally, I rather liked the lad, though he was a bit harum-scarum. I dare say he's sobered up with time – and marriage. It's odd that they can't find the will. But, if it was made at the time of the rumpus, it's bound to be in Haviland's favour.'

'I think Haviland thinks so,' said Wimsey. 'His manner seemed to convey a chastened satisfaction. I expect the discreet Graham made it fairly clear that the advantage was not with the unspeakable Martin.'

The following morning turned out fine, and Wimsey, who was supposed to be enjoying a rest-and-fresh-air cure in Little Doddering, petitioned for a further loan of Polly Flinders. His host consented with pleasure, and only regretted that he could not accompany his guest, being booked to attend a Board of Guardians' meeting in connection with the workhouse.

'But you could go up and get a good blow on the common,' he suggested. 'Why not go round by Petering Friars, turn off across the common till you get to Dead Man's Post, and come back by the Frimpton road? It makes a very pleasant round – about nineteen miles. You'll be back in nice time for lunch if you take it easy.'

Wimsey fell in with the plan – the more readily that it exactly coincided with his own inward purpose. He had a reason for wishing to ride over the Frimpton road by daylight.

'You'll be careful about Dead Man's Post,' said Mrs Frobisher-Pym a little anxiously. 'The horses have a way of shying at it. I don't know why. People say, of course—'

'All nonsense,' said her husband. 'The villagers dislike the place and that makes the horses nervous. It's remarkable how a rider's feelings communicate themselves to his mount. I've never had any trouble at Dead Man's Post.'

It was a quiet and pretty road, even on a November day, that led to Petering Friars. Jogging down the winding Essex lanes in the wintry sunshine, Wimsey felt soothed and happy. A good burst across the common raised his spirits to exhilaration pitch. He had entirely forgotten Dead Man's Post and its uncanny reputation, when a violent start and swerve, so sudden that it nearly unseated him, recalled him to what he was doing. With some difficulty, he controlled Polly Flinders, and brought her to a standstill.

He was at the highest point of the common, following a bridle-path which was bordered on each side by gorse and dead bracken. A little way ahead of him another bridle-path seemed to run into it, and at the junction of the two was something which he had vaguely imagined to be a decayed signpost. Certainly it was short and thick for a signpost, and had no arms. It appeared, however, to bear some sort of inscription on the face that was turned towards him.

He soothed the mare, and urged her gently towards the post. She took a few hesitating steps, and plunged sideways, snorting and shivering.

'Queer!' said Wimsey. 'If this is my state of mind communicating itself to my mount, I'd better see a doctor. My nerves must be in a rotten state. Come up, old lady! What's the matter with you?'

Polly Flinders, apologetic but determined, refused to budge. He urged her gently with his heel. She sidled away, with ears laid back, and he saw the white of a protesting eye. He slipped from the saddle, and, putting his hand through the bridle, endeavoured to lead her forward. After a little persuasion, the mare followed him, with stretched neck and treading as though on egg-shells. After a dozen hesitating paces, she stopped again, trembling in all her limbs. He put his hand on her neck and found it wet with sweat.

'Damn it all!' said Wimsey. 'Look here, I'm jolly well going to read what's on that post. If you won't come, will you stand still?'

He dropped the bridle. The mare stood quietly, with hanging head. He left her and went forward, glancing back from time to time to see that she showed no disposition to bolt. She stood quietly enough, however, only shifting her feet uneasily.

Wimsey walked up to the post. It was a stout pillar of ancient oak, newly painted white. The inscription, too, had been recently blacked in. It read:

ON THIS SPOT
GEORGE WINTER
WAS FOULLY MURTHERED
IN DEFENSE OF
HIS MASTER'S GOODS
BY BLACK RALPH
OF HERRIOTTING
WHO WAS AFTERWARD
HANGED IN CHAINS
ON THE PLACE OF HIS CRIME
9 NOVEMBER 1674

FEAR JUSTICE

'And very nice, too,' said Wimsey. 'Dead Man's Post without a doubt. Polly Flinders seems to share the local feeling about the place. Well, Polly, if them's your sentiments, I won't do violence to them. But may I ask why, if you're so sensitive about a mere post, you should swallow a death-coach and four headless horses with such hardened equanimity?'

The mare took the shoulder of his jacket gently between her lips and mumbled at it.

'Just so,' said Wimsey. 'I perfectly understand. You would if you could, but you really can't. But those horses, Polly – did they bring with them no brimstone blast from the nethermost pit? Can it be that they really exuded nothing but an honest and familiar smell of stables?'

He mounted, and, turning Polly's head to the right, guided her in a circle, so as to give Dead Man's Post a wide berth before striking the path again.

'The supernatural explanation is, I think, excluded. Not on *a priori* grounds, which would be unsound, but on the evidence of Polly's senses. There remain the alternatives of whisky and jiggery-pokery. Further investigation seems called for.'

He continued to muse as the mare moved quietly forward.

'Supposing I wanted, for some reason, to scare the neighbourhood with the apparition of a coach and headless horses, I should choose a dark, rainy night. Good! It was that kind of night. Now, if I took black horses and painted their bodies white – poor devils! What a state they'd be in. No. How do they do these Maskelyne-and-Devant stunts where they cut off people's heads? White horses, of course – and black felt clothing over their heads. Right! And luminous paint on the harness, with a touch here and there on their bodies, to make good contrast and ensure that the whole show wasn't invisible. No difficulty about that. But they must go silently. Well, why not? Four stout black cloth bags filled with bran, drawn well up and tied round the fetlocks would make any horse go quietly enough, especially if there was a bit of a wind going. Rags round the bridle-rings to prevent clinking, and round the ends of the traces to keep 'em from squeaking. Give 'em a coachman in a white coat and a black mask, hitch 'em to a rubber-tyred fly, picked out with phosphorus and well-oiled at the joints – and I swear I'd make something quite ghostly enough to startle a rather well-irrigated gentleman on a lonely road at half-past two in the morning.'

He was pleased with this thought, and tapped his boot cheerfully with his whip.

'But damn it all! They never passed me again. Where did

they go to? A coach-and-horses can't vanish into thin air, you know. There must be a side-road after all – or else, Polly Flinders, you've been pulling my leg all the time.'

The bridle-path eventually debouched upon the highway at the now familiar fork where Wimsey had met the policeman. As he slowly ambled homewards, his lordship scanned the left-hand hedgerow, looking for the lane which surely must exist. But nothing rewarded his search. Enclosed fields with padlocked gates presented the only breaks in the hedge, till he again found himself looking down the avenue of trees up which the death-coach had come galloping two nights before.

'Damn!' said Wimsey.

It occurred to him for the first time that the coach might perhaps have turned round and gone back through Little Doddering. Certainly it had been seen by Little Doddering Church on Wednesday. But on that occasion, also, it had galloped off in the direction of Frimpton. In fact, thinking it over, Wimsey concluded that it had approached from Frimpton, gone round the church – widdershins, naturally – by the Back Lane, and returned by the high-road whence it came. But in that case—

'Turn again, Whittington,' said Wimsey, and Polly Flinders rotated obediently in the road. 'Through one of those fields it went, or I'm a Dutchman.'

He pulled Polly into a slow walk, and passed along the strip of grass at the right-hand side, staring at the ground as though he were an Aberdonian who had lost a sixpence.

The first gate led into a ploughed field, harrowed smooth and sown with autumn wheat. It was clear that no wheeled thing had been across it for many weeks. The second gate looked more promising. It gave upon fallow ground, and the entrance was seamed with innumerable wheel-ruts. On further examination, however, it was clear that this was the one and only gate. It seemed unlikely that the mysterious coach should have been taken into a field from which there was no way out. Wimsey decided to seek farther.

The third gate was in bad repair. It sagged heavily from its hinges; the hasp was gone, and gate and post had been secured with elaborate twists of wire. Wimsey dismounted and examined these, convincing himself that their rusty surface had not been recently disturbed.

There remained only two more gates before he came to the cross-roads. One led into plough again, where the dark ridge-and-furrow showed no sign of disturbance, but at sight of the last gate Wimsey's heart gave a leap.

There was plough-land here also, but round the edge of the field ran a wide, beaten path, rutted and water-logged. The gate was not locked, but opened simply with a spring catch. Wimsey examined the approach. Among the wide ruts made by farm-wagons was the track of four narrow wheels – the unmistakable prints of rubber tyres. He pushed the gate open and passed through.

The path skirted two sides of the plough; then came another gate and another field, containing a long barrow of mangold wurzels and a couple of barns. At the sound of Polly's hoofs, a man emerged from the nearest barn, with a paint-brush in his hand, and stood watching Wimsey's approach.

'Morning!' said the latter genially.

'Morning, sir.'

'Fine day after the rain.'

'Yes, it is, sir.'

'I hope I'm not trespassing?'

'Where was you wanting to go, sir?'

'I thought, as a matter of fact – hullo!'

'Anything wrong, sir?'

Wimsey shifted in the saddle.

'I fancy this girth's slipped a bit. It's a new one.' (This was a fact.) 'Better have a look.'

The man advanced to investigate, but Wimsey had dismounted and was tugging at the strap, with his head under the mare's belly.

'Yes, it wants taking up a trifle. Oh! Thanks most awfully. Is this a short cut to Abbotts Bolton, by the way?'

'Not to the village, sir, though you can get through this way. It comes out by Mr Mortimer's stables.'

'Ah, yes. This his land?'

'No, sir, it's Mr Topham's land, but Mr Mortimer rents this field and the next for fodder.'

'Oh, yes.' Wimsey peered across the hedge. 'Lucerne, I suppose. Or clover.'

'Clover, sir. And the mangolds is for the cattle.'

'Oh – Mr Mortimer keeps cattle as well as horses?'

'Yes, sir.'

'Very jolly. Have a gasper?' Wimsey had sidled across to the barn in his interest, and was gazing absently into its dark interior. It contained a number of farm implements and a black fly of antique construction, which seemed to be undergoing renovation with black varnish. Wimsey pulled some vestas from his pocket. The box was apparently damp, for, after one or two vain attempts he abandoned it, and struck a match on the wall of the barn. The flame, lighting up the ancient fly, showed it to be incongruously fitted with rubber tyres.

'Very fine stud, Mr Mortimer's, I understand,' said Wimsey carelessly.

'Yes, sir, very fine indeed.'

'I suppose he hasn't any greys, by any chance. My mother – queenly woman, Victorian ideas, and all that – is rather keen on greys. Sports a carriage and pay-ah, don't you know.'

'Yes, sir? Well, Mr Mortimer would be able to suit the lady, I think, sir. He has several greys.'

'No? Has he though? I must really go over and see him. Is it far?'

'Matter of five or six mile by the fields, sir.'

Wimsey looked at his watch.

'Oh, dear! I'm really afraid it's too far for this morning. I absolutely promised to get back to lunch. I must come over another day. Thanks so much. Is that girth right now? Oh, really, I'm immensely obliged. Get yourself a drink, won't you – and tell Mr Mortimer not to sell his greys till I've seen them. Well, *good* morning, and many thanks.'

He set Polly Flinders on the homeward path and trotted gently away. Not till he was out of sight of the barn did he pull up and, stooping from the saddle, thoughtfully examine his boots. They were liberally plastered with bran.

'I must have picked it up in the barn,' said Wimsey. 'Curious, if true. Why should Mr Mortimer be lashing the stuffing out of his greys in an old fly at dead of night – and with muffled hoofs and no heads to boot? It's not a kind thing to do. It frightened Plunkett very much. It made me think I was drunk – a thought I hate to think. Ought I to tell the police? Are Mr Mortimer's jokes any business of mine? What do *you* think, Polly?'

The mare, hearing her name, energetically shook her head. 'You think not? Perhaps you are right. Let us say that Mr Mortimer did it for a wager. Who am I to interfere with his amusements? All the same,' added his lordship, 'I'm glad to know it wasn't Lumsden's whisky.'

'This is the library,' said Haviland, ushering in his guests. 'A fine room – and a fine collection of books, I'm told, though literature isn't much in my line. It wasn't much in the governor's line, either, I'm afraid. The place wants doing up, as you see. I don't know whether Martin will take it in hand. It's a job that'll cost money, of course.'

Wimsey shivered a little as he gazed round – more from sympathy than from cold, though a white November fog lay curled against the tall windows and filtered damply through the frames.

A long, mouldering room, in the frigid neo-classical style, the library was melancholy enough in the sunless grey afternoon, even without the signs of neglect which wrung the book-collector's heart. The walls, panelled to half their height with book-cases, ran up in plaster to the moulded ceiling. Damp had blotched them into grotesque shapes, and here and there were ugly cracks and squamous patches, from which the plaster had fallen in yellowish flakes. A wet chill seemed to ooze from the books, from the calf bindings peeling and perishing, from the stains of greenish mildew which spread horridly from volume to volume. The curious musty odour of decayed leather and damp paper added to the general cheerlessness of the atmosphere.

'Oh, dear, dear!' said Wimsey, peering dismally into this sepulchre of forgotten learning. With his shoulders hunched like the neck-feathers of a chilly bird, with his long nose and half-shut eyes, he resembled a dilapidated heron, brooding over the stagnation of a wintry pool.

'What a freezing-cold place!' exclaimed Mrs Hancock. 'You really ought to scold Mrs Lovall, Mr Burdock. When she was put in here as caretaker, I said to my husband – didn't I, Philip? – that your father had chosen the laziest woman in Little Doddering. She ought to have kept up big fires here, *at least* twice a week! It's really shameful, the way she has let things go.'

'Yes, isn't it?' agreed Haviland.

Wimsey said nothing. He was nosing along the shelves, every now and then taking a volume down and glancing at it.

'It was always rather a depressing room,' went on Haviland. 'I remember, when I was a kid, it used to overawe me rather. Martin and I used to browse about among the books, you know, but I think we were always afraid that something or somebody would stalk out upon us from the dark corners. What's that you've got there, Lord Peter? Oh, *Foxe's Book of Martyrs*. Dear me! How those pictures did terrify me in the old days! And there was a *Pilgrim's Progress*, with a most alarming picture of Apollyon straddling over the whole breadth of the way, which gave me many nightmares. Let me see. It used to live over in this bay, I think. Yes, here it is. How it does bring it all back, to be sure! Is it valuable, by the way?'

'No, not really. But this first edition of Burton is worth money; badly spotted, though – you'd better send it to be cleaned. And this is an extremely fine Boccaccio; take care of it.'

'John Boccace – *The Dance of Machabree*. It's a good title, anyhow. Is that the same Boccaccio that wrote the naughty stories?'

'Yes,' said Wimsey, a little shortly. He resented this attitude towards Boccaccio.

'Never read them,' said Haviland, with a wink at his wife, 'but I've seen 'em in the windows of those surgical shops – so I suppose they're naughty, eh? The vicar's looking shocked.'

'Oh, not at all,' said Mr Hancock, with a conscientious assumption of broad-mindedness. '*Et ego in Arcadia* – that is to say, one doesn't enter the Church without undergoing a classical education, and making the acquaintance of much more worldly authors even than Boccaccio. Those woodcuts are very fine, to my uninstructed eye.'

'Very fine indeed,' said Wimsey.

'There's another old book I remember, with jolly pictures,' said Haviland. 'A chronicle of some sort – what's 'is name – place in Germany – *you* know – where that hangman came from. They published his diary the other day. I read it, but it wasn't really exciting; not half as gruesome as old Harrison Ainsworth. What's the name of the place?'

'Nüremberg?' suggested Wimsey.

'That's it, of course – the *Nüremberg Chronicle*. I wonder if that's still in its old place. It was over here by the window, if I remember rightly.'

He led the way to the end of one of the bays, which ran up close against a window. Here the damp seemed to have done its worst. A pane of glass was broken, and rain had blown in.

'Now where has it gone to? A big book, it was, with a stamped leather binding. I'd like to see the old *Chronicle* again. I haven't set eyes on it for donkey's years.'

His glance roamed vaguely over the shelves. Wimsey, with the booklover's instinct, was the first to spot the *Chronicle*, wedged at the extreme end of the shelf, against the outer wall. He hitched his finger into the top edge of the spine, but finding that the rotting leather was ready to crumble at a touch, he dislodged a neighbouring book and drew the *Chronicle* gently out, using his whole hand.

'Here he is – in pretty bad condition, I'm afraid. Hullo!'

As he drew the book away from the wall, a piece of folded parchment came away with it and fell at his feet. He stooped and picked it up.

'I say, Burdock – isn't this what you've been looking for?'

Haviland Burdock, who had been rooting about on one of the lower shelves, straightened himself quickly, his face red from stooping.

'By Jove!' he said, turning first redder and then pale with excitement. 'Look at this, Winnie. It's the governor's will. What an extraordinary thing! Whoever would have thought of looking for it here, of all places?'

'Is it really the will?' cried Mrs Hancock.

'No doubt about it, I should say,' observed Wimsey coolly. 'Last Will and Testament of Simon Burdock.' He stood, turning the grimy document over and over in his hands, looking from the endorsement to the plain side of the folded parchment.

'Well, well!' said Mr Hancock. 'How strange! It seems almost providential that you should have taken that book down.'

'What does the will say?' demanded Mrs Burdock, in some excitement.

'I beg your pardon,' said Wimsey, handing it over to her. 'Yes, as you say, Mr Hancock, it does almost seem as if I was meant to find it.' He glanced down again at the *Chronicle*, mournfully tracing with his finger the outline of a damp stain which had rotted the cover and spread to the inner pages, almost obliterating the colophon.

Haviland Burdock, meanwhile, had spread the will out on the nearest table. His wife leaned over his shoulder. The Hancocks, barely controlling their curiosity, stood near, awaiting the result. Wimsey, with an elaborate pretence of non-interference in this family matter, examined the wall against which the *Chronicle* had stood, feeling its moist surface and examining the damp-stains. They had assumed the appearance of a grinning face. He compared them with the corresponding mark on the book, and shook his head desolately over the damage.

Mr Frobisher-Pym, who had wandered away some time before and was absorbed in an ancient book of Farriery, now approached, and enquired what the excitement was about.

'Listen to this!' cried Haviland. His voice was quiet, but a suppressed triumph throbbed in it and glittered from his eyes.

'"I bequeath everything of which I die possessed" – there's a lot of enumeration of properties here, which doesn't matter – "to my eldest son, Martin"—'

Mr Frobisher-Pym whistled.

'Listen! "To my eldest son Martin, for so long as my body shall remain above ground. But so soon as I am buried, I direct that the whole of this property shall revert to my younger son Haviland absolutely"—'

'Good God!' said Mr Frobisher-Pym.

'There's a lot more,' said Haviland, 'but that's the gist of it.'

'Let me see,' said the magistrate.

He took the will from Haviland, and read it through with a frowning face.

'That's right,' he said. 'No possible doubt about it. Martin has had his property and lost it again. How very curious. Up till yesterday everything belonged to him, though nobody knew it. Now it is all yours, Burdock. This certainly is the strangest will I ever saw. Just fancy that. Martin the heir, up to the time of the funeral. And now – well, Burdock, I must congratulate you.'

'Thank you,' said Haviland. 'It is very unexpected.' He laughed unsteadily.

'But what a queer idea!' cried Mrs Burdock. 'Suppose Martin had been at home. It almost seems a mercy that he wasn't, doesn't it? I mean, it would all have been so awkward. What would have happened if he had tried to stop the funeral, for instance?'

'Yes,' said Mrs Hancock. 'Could he have done anything? Who decides about funerals?'

'The executors, as a rule,' said Mr Frobisher-Pym.

'Who are the executors in this case?' enquired Wimsey.

'I don't know. Let me see.' Mr Frobisher-Pym examined the document again. 'Ah, yes! Here we are. "I appoint my two sons, Martin and Haviland, joint executors of this my will." What an extraordinary arrangement.'

'I call it a wicked, un-Christian arrangement,' cried Mrs Hancock. 'It might have caused dreadful mischief if the will hadn't been – quite providentially – lost!'

'Hush, my dear!' said her husband.

'I'm afraid,' said Haviland grimly, 'that that was my father's idea. It's no use my pretending he wasn't spiteful; he was, and I believe he hated both Martin and me like poison.'

'Don't say that,' pleaded the vicar.

'I do say it. He made our lives a burden to us, and he obviously wanted to go on making them a burden after he was dead. If he'd seen us cutting each other's throats, he'd only have been too pleased. Come, vicar, it's no use pretending. He hated our mother and was jealous of us. Everybody knows that. It probably pleased his unpleasant sense of humour to think of us squabbling over his body. Fortunately, he overreached himself when he hid the will here. He's buried now, and the problem settles itself.'

'Are you quite sure of that?' said Wimsey.

'Why, of course,' said the magistrate. 'The property goes to Mr Haviland Burdock as soon as his father's body is underground. Well, his father was buried yesterday.'

'But are you sure of *that*?' repeated Wimsey. He looked from one to the other quizzically, his long lips curling into something like a grin.

'Sure of that?' exclaimed the vicar. 'My dear Lord Peter, you were present at the funeral. You saw him buried yourself.'

'I saw his coffin buried,' said Wimsey mildly. 'That the body was in it is merely an unverified inference.'

'I think,' said Mr Frobisher-Pym, 'this is rather an unseemly kind of jest. There is no reason to imagine that the body was not in the coffin.'

'I saw it in the coffin,' said Haviland, 'and so did my wife.'

'And so did I,' said the vicar. 'I was present when it was transferred from the temporary shell in which it crossed over from the States to a permanent lead-and-oak coffin provided by Joliffe. And, if further witnesses are necessary, you can easily get Joliffe himself and his men, who put the body in and screwed it down.'

'Just so,' said Wimsey. 'I'm not denying that the body was in the coffin when the coffin was placed in the chapel. I only doubt whether it was there when it was put in the ground.'

'That is a most unheard-of suggestion to make, Lord Peter,' said Mr Frobisher-Pym, with severity. 'May I ask if you have anything to go upon? And, if the body is not in the grave, perhaps you wouldn't mind telling us where you imagine it to be?'

'Not at all,' said Wimsey. He perched himself on the edge of the table and sat, swinging his legs and looking down at his own hands, as he ticked his points off on his fingers.

'I think,' he said, 'that this story begins with young Raw-linson. He is a clerk in the office of Mr Graham, who drew up this will, and I fancy he knows something about its conditions. So, of course, does Mr Graham, but I don't somehow suspect *him* of being mixed up in this. From what I can hear, he is not a man to take sides – or not Mr Martin's side, at any rate.

'When the news of Mr Burdock's death was cabled over from the States, I think young Rawlinson remembered the terms of the will, and considered that Mr Martin – being abroad and all that – would be rather at a disadvantage. Rawlinson must be rather attached to your brother, by the way—'

'Martin always had a way of picking up good-for-nothing youths and wasting his time with them,' agreed Haviland sulkily.

The vicar seemed to feel that this statement needed some amendment, and murmured that he had always heard how good Martin was with the village lads.

'Quite so,' said Wimsey. 'Well, I think young Rawlinson wanted to give Martin an equal chance of securing the legacy, don't you see. He didn't like to say anything about the will – which might or might not turn up – and possibly he thought that even if it did turn up there might be difficulties. Well, anyway, he decided that the best thing to do was to steal the body and keep it above ground till Martin came home to see to things himself.'

'This is an extraordinary accusation,' began Mr Frobisher-Pym.

'I dare say I'm mistaken,' said Wimsey, 'but it's just my idea. It makes a damn good story, anyhow – you see! Well, then, young Rawlinson saw that this was too big a job to carry out alone, so he looked round for somebody to help him. And he pitched on Mr Mortimer.'

'Mortimer?'

'I don't know Mr Mortimer personally, but he seems to be a sportin' sort of customer from what I can hear, with certain facilities which everybody hasn't got. Young Rawlinson and Mortimer put their heads together and worked out a plan of action. Of course, Mr Hancock, you helped them enormously with this lying-in-state idea of yours. Without that, I don't know if they could have worked it.'

Mr Hancock made an embarrassed clucking sound.

'The idea was this. Mortimer was to provide an antique fly and four white horses, made up with luminous paint and black cloth to represent the Burdock death-coach. The advantage of that idea was that nobody would feel inclined to inspect the turn-out too closely if they saw it hangin' round the churchyard at unearthly hours. Meanwhile, young Rawlinson had to get himself accepted as a watcher for the chapel, and to find a sporting companion to watch with him and take a hand in the game. He fixed things up with the publican-fellow, and spun a tale for Mr Hancock, so as to get the vigil from four to six. Didn't it strike you as odd, Mr Hancock, that he should be so keen to come all the way from Herriotting?'

'I am accustomed to find keenness in my congregation,' said Mr Hancock stiffly.

'Yes, but Rawlinson didn't belong to your congregation. Anyway it was all worked out, and there was a dress-rehearsal on the Wednesday night, which frightened your man Plunkett into fits, sir.'

'If I thought this was true—' said Mr Frobisher-Pym.

'On Thursday night,' pursued Wimsey, 'the conspirators were ready, hidden in the chancel at two in the morning.

They waited till Mrs and Miss Hancock had taken their places, and then made a row to attract their attention. When the ladies courageously advanced to find out what was up, they popped out and bundled 'em into the vestry.'

'Good gracious!' said Mrs Hancock.

'That was when the death-coach affair was timed to drive up to the south door. It came round the Back Lane, I fancy, though I can't be sure. Then Mortimer and the other two took the embalmed body out of the coffin and filled its place up with bags of sawdust. I know it was sawdust, because I found the remains of it on the Lady-chapel floor in the morning. They put the body in the fly, and Mortimer drove off with it. They passed me on the Herriotting Road at half-past two, so they can't have wasted much time over the job. Mortimer may have been alone, or possibly he had someone with him to see to the body while he himself did the headless coachman business in a black mask. I'm not certain about that. They drove through the last gate before you come to the fork at Frimpton, and went across the fields to Mortimer's barn. They left the fly there – I know that, because I saw it, and I saw the bran they used to muffle the horses' hoofs, too. I expect they took it on from there in a car, and fetched the horses up next day – but that's a detail. I don't know, either, where they took the body to, but I expect, if you went and asked Mortimer about it, he would be able to assure you that it was still above ground.'

Wimsey paused. Mr Frobisher-Pym and the Hancocks were looking only puzzled and angry, but Haviland's face was green. Mrs Haviland showed a red, painted spot on each cheek, and her mouth was haggard. Wimsey picked up the

Nüremberg Chronicle and caressed its covers thoughtfully as he went on.

'Meanwhile, of course, young Rawlinson and his companion were doing the camouflage in the church, to give the idea of a Protestant outrage. Having fixed everything up neat and pretty, all they had to do was to lock themselves up in the furnace-house and chuck the key through the window. You'll probably find it there, Mr Hancock, if you care to look. Didn't you think that story of an assault by two or three men was a bit thin? Hubbard is a hefty great fellow, and Rawlinson's a sturdy lad – and yet, on their own showing, they were bundled into a coal-hole like helpless infants, without a scratch on either of 'em. Look for the men in buckram, my dear sir, look for the men in buckram!'

'Look here, Wimsey, are you sure you're not romancing?' said Mr Frobisher-Pym. 'One would need some very clear proof before—'

'Certainly,' said Wimsey. 'Get a Home Office order. Open the grave. You'll soon see whether it's true or whether it's just my diseased imagination.'

'I think this whole conversation is disgusting,' cried Mrs Burdock. 'Don't listen to it, Haviland. Anything more heartless on the day after father's funeral than sitting here and inventing such a revolting story I simply can't imagine. It is not worth paying a moment's attention to. You will certainly not permit your father's body to be disturbed. It's horrible. It's a desecration.'

'It is very unpleasant indeed,' said Mr Frobisher-Pym gravely, 'but if Lord Peter is seriously putting forward this astonishing theory, which I can scarcely credit—'

Wimsey shrugged his shoulders.

'—then I feel bound to remind you, Mr Burdock, that your brother, when he returns, may insist on having the matter investigated.'

'But he can't, can he?' said Mrs Burdock.

'Of course he can, Winnie,' snapped her husband savagely. 'He's an executor. He has as much right to have the governor dug up as I have to forbid it. Don't be a fool.'

'If Martin had any decency, he would forbid it, too,' said Mrs Burdock.

'Oh, well!' said Mrs Hancock, 'shocking as it may seem, there's the money to be considered. Mr Martin might think it a duty to his wife, and his family, if he should ever have any—'

'The whole thing is preposterous,' said Haviland decidedly. 'I don't believe a word of it. If I did, naturally I should be the first person to take action in the matter – not only in justice to Martin, but on my own account. But if you ask me to believe that a responsible man like Mortimer would purloin a corpse and desecrate a church – the thing only has to be put into plain words to show how absurd and unthinkable it is. I suppose Lord Peter Wimsey, who consorts, as I understand, with criminals and police officers, finds the idea conceivable. I can only say that I do not. I am sorry that his mind should have become so blunted to all decent feeling. That's all. Good afternoon.'

Mr Frobisher-Pym jumped up.

'Come, come, Burdock, don't take that attitude. I am sure Lord Peter intended no discourtesy. I must say I think he's all wrong, but, 'pon my soul, things have been so disturbed in the village these last few days, I'm not surprised anybody should think there was something behind it. Now, let's forget about it – and hadn't we better be moving out of this terribly cold room? It's nearly dinner-time. Bless me, what will Agatha think of us?'

Wimsey held out his hand to Burdock, who took it reluctantly.

'I'm sorry,' said Wimsey. 'I suffer from hypertrophy of the imagination, y'know. Over-stimulation of the thyroid probably. Don't mind me. I apologise, and all that.'

'I don't think, Lord Peter,' said Mrs Burdock acidly, 'you ought to exercise your imagination at the expense of good taste.'

Wimsey followed her from the room in some confusion. Indeed, he was so disturbed that he carried away the *Nüremberg Chronicle* beneath his arm, which was an odd thing for him to do under the circumstances.

'I am gravely distressed,' said Mr Hancock.

He had come over, after Sunday evening service, to call upon the Frobisher-Pyms. He sat upright on his chair, his thin face flushed with anxiety.

'I could never have believed such a thing of Hubbard. It has been a grievous shock to me. It is not only the great wickedness of stealing a dead body from the very precincts of the church, though that is grave enough. It is the sad hypocrisy of his behaviour – the mockery of sacred things – the making use of the holy services of his religion to further worldly ends. He actually attended the funeral, Mr Frobisher-Pym, and exhibited every sign of grief and respect. Even now he hardly seems to realise the sinfulness of his conduct. I feel it very much, as a priest and as a pastor – very much indeed.'

'Oh, well, Hancock,' said Mr Frobisher-Pym, 'you must make allowances, you know. Hubbard's not a bad fellow, but you can't expect refinement of feeling from a man of his class. The point is, what are we to do about it? Mr Burdock must be told, of course. It's a most awkward situation. Dear me! Hubbard confessed the whole conspiracy, you say? How did he come to do that?'

'I taxed him with it,' said the parson. 'When I came to think over Lord Peter Wimsey's remarks, I was troubled in my mind. It seemed to me – I cannot say why – that there might be some truth in the story, wild as it appeared. I was so worried about it that I swept the floor of the Lady-chapel myself last night, and I found quite a quantity of sawdust among the sweepings. That led me to search for the key of the furnace-house, and I discovered it in some bushes at a little distance – in fact, within a stone's throw – of the furnace-house window. I sought guidance in prayer – and from my wife, whose judgment I greatly respect – and I made up my mind to speak to Hubbard after Mass. It was a great relief to me that he did not present himself at Early Celebration. Feeling as I did, I should have had scruples.'

'Just so, just so,' said the magistrate, a little impatiently. 'Well, you taxed him with it, and he confessed?'

'He did. I am sorry to say he showed no remorse at all. He even laughed. It was a most painful interview.'

'I am sure it must have been,' said Mrs Frobisher-Pym sympathetically.

'We must go and see Mr Burdock,' said the magistrate, rising. 'Whatever old Burdock may or may not have intended by that iniquitous will of his, it's quite evident that Hubbard and Mortimer and Rawlinson were entirely in the wrong. Upon my word, I've no idea whether it's an indictable offence to steal a body. I must look it up. But I should say it was. If there is any property in a corpse, it must belong to the family or the executors. And in any case, it's sacrilege, to say nothing of the scandal in the parish. I must say, Hancock, it won't do us any good in the eyes of the Nonconformists. However, no doubt you realise that. Well, it's an unpleasant job, and the sooner we tackle it the better. I'll run over to the vicarage with you and help you to break it to the Burdocks. How about you, Wimsey? You were right, after all, and I think Burdock owes you an apology.'

'Oh, I'll keep out of it,' said Wimsey. 'I shan't be exactly *persona grata*, don't you know. It's going to mean a deuce of a big financial loss to the Haviland Burdocks.'

'So it is. Most unpleasant. Well, perhaps you're right. Come along, vicar.'

Wimsey and his hostess sat discussing the matter by the fire for half an hour or so, when Mr Frobisher-Pym suddenly put his head in and said:

'I say, Wimsey – we're all going over to Mortimer's. I wish you'd come and drive the car. Merridew always has the day off on Sunday, and I don't care about driving at night, particularly in this fog.'

'Right you are,' said Wimsey. He ran upstairs, and came down in a few moments wearing a heavy leather flying-coat, and with a parcel under his arm. He greeted the Burdocks briefly, climbed into the driving-seat, and was soon steering cautiously through the mist along the Herriotting Road.

He smiled a little grimly to himself as they came up under the trees to the spot where the phantom coach had passed him. As they passed the gate through which the ingenious apparition had vanished, he indulged himself by pointing it out, and was rewarded by hearing a snarl from Haviland. At the well-remembered fork, he took the right-hand turning into Frimpton and drove steadily for six miles or so, till a warning shout from Mr Frobisher-Pym summoned him to look out for the turning up to Mortimer's.

Mr Mortimer's house, with its extensive stabling and farm buildings, stood about two miles back from the main road. In the darkness Wimsey could see little of it; but he noticed that the ground-floor windows were all lit up, and, when the door opened to the magistrate's imperative ring, a loud burst of laughter from the interior gave evidence that Mr Mortimer was not taking his misdoings too seriously.

'Is Mr Mortimer at home?' demanded Mr Frobisher-Pym, in the tone of a man not to be trifled with.

'Yes, sir. Will you come in, please?'

They stepped into a large, old-fashioned hall, brilliantly lit, and made cosy with a heavy oak screen across the door. As Wimsey advanced, blinking, from the darkness, he saw a large, thick-set man, with a ruddy face, advancing with hand outstretched in welcome.

'Frobisher-Pym! By Jove! How decent of you to come over! We've got some old friends of yours here. Oh!' (in a slightly altered tone) 'Burdock! Well, well—'

'Damn you!' said Haviland Burdock, thrusting furiously

past the magistrate, who was trying to hold him back. 'Damn you, you swine! Chuck this bloody farce. What have you done with the body?'

'The body, eh?' said Mr Mortimer, retreating in some confusion.

'Yes, curse you! Your friend Hubbard's split. It's no good denying it. What the devil do you mean by it? You've got the body here somewhere. Where is it? Hand it over!'

He strode threateningly round the screen into the lamplight. A tall, thin man rose up unexpectedly from the depths of an armchair and confronted him.

'Hold hard, old man!'

'Good God!' said Haviland, stepping heavily back on Wimsey's toes. 'Martin!'

'Sure,' said the other. 'Here I am. Come back like a bad half-penny. How are you?'

'So *you're* at the bottom of this!' stormed Haviland. 'I might have known it. You damned, dirty hound! I suppose you think it's decent to drag your father out of his coffin and tote him about the country like a circus. It's degrading. It's disgusting. It's abominable. You must be perfectly dead to all decent feeling. You don't deny it, I suppose?'

'I say, Burdock!' expostulated Mortimer.

'Shut up, curse you!' said Haviland. 'I'll deal with you in a minute. Now, look here, Martin, I'm not going to stand any more of this disgraceful behaviour. You'll give up that body, and—'

'Just a moment, just a moment,' said Martin. He stood, smiling a little, his hands thrust into the pockets of his dinner-jacket. 'This *éclaircissement* seems to be rather public.

115

Who are all these people? Oh, it's the vicar, I see. I'm afraid we owe you a little explanation, vicar. And, er—'

'This is Lord Peter Wimsey,' put in Mr Frobisher-Pym, 'who discovered your – I'm afraid, Burdock, I must agree with your brother in calling it your disgraceful plot.'

'Oh, Lord!' said Martin. 'I say, Mortimer, you didn't know you were up against Lord Peter Wimsey, did you? No wonder the cat got out of the bag. The man's known to be a perfect Sherlock. However, I seem to have got home at the crucial moment, so there's no harm done. Diana, this is Lord Peter Wimsey – my wife.'

A young and pretty woman in a black evening dress greeted Wimsey with a shy smile, and turned deprecatingly to her brother-in-law.

'Haviland, we want to explain—'

He paid no attention to her.

'Now then, Martin, the game's up.'

'I think it is, Haviland. But why make all this racket?'

'Racket! I like that. You take your own father's body out of its coffin—'

'No, no, Haviland. I knew nothing about it. I swear that. I only got the news of his death a few days ago. We were right out in the wilds, filming a show in the Pyrenees, and I came straight back as soon as I could get away. Mortimer here, with Rawlinson and Hubbard, staged the whole show by themselves. I never heard a word about it till yesterday morning in Paris, when I found his letter waiting at my old digs. Honestly, Haviland, I had nothing to do with it. Why should I? I didn't need to.'

'What do you mean?'

'Well, if I'd been here, I should only have had to speak to stop the funeral altogether. Why on earth should I have gone to the trouble of stealing the body? Quite apart from the irreverence and all that. As it is, when Mortimer told me about it, I must say I was a bit revolted at the idea, though I appreciated the kindness and the trouble they'd been to on my account. I think Mr Hancock has most cause for wrath, really. But Mortimer has been as careful as possible, sir – really he has. He has placed the old governor quite reverently and decently in what used to be the chapel, and put flowers round him and so on. You will be quite satisfied, I'm sure.'

'Yes, yes,' said Mortimer. 'No disrespect intended, don't you know. Come and see him.'

'This is dreadful,' said the vicar helplessly.

'They had to do the best they could, don't you see, in my absence,' said Martin. 'As soon as I can, I'll make proper arrangements for a suitable tomb – above ground, of course. Or possibly cremation would fit the case.'

'What!' gasped Haviland. 'Do you mean to say you imagine I'm going to let my father stay unburied, simply because of your disgusting greed about money?'

'My dear chap, do you think I'm going to let you put him underground, simply to enable you to grab my property?'

'I'm the executor of his will, and I say he shall be buried, whether you like it or not!'

'And *I'm* an executor too – and I say he shan't be buried. He can be kept absolutely decently above ground, and he shall be.'

'But hear me,' said the vicar, distracted between these two disagreeable and angry young men.

'I'll see what Graham says about you,' bawled Haviland.

'Oh, yes – the honest lawyer, Graham,' sneered Martin. '*He* knew what was in the will, didn't he? I suppose he didn't mention it to *you*, by any chance?'

'He did not,' retorted Haviland. 'He knew too well the sort of skunk *you* were to say anything about it. Not content with disgracing us with your miserable, blackmailing marriage—'

'Mr Burdock, Mr Burdock—'

'Take care, Haviland!'

'You have no more decency—'

'Stop it!'

'Than to steal your father's body and my money so that you and your damned wife can carry on your loose-living, beastly ways with a parcel of film-actors and chorus-girls—'

'Now then, Haviland. Keep your tongue off my wife and my friends. How about your own? Somebody told me Winnie'd been going the pace pretty well – next door to bankruptcy, aren't you, with the gees and the tables and God knows what! No wonder you want to do your brother out of his money. I never thought much of you, Haviland, but by God—'

'One moment!'

Mr Frobisher-Pym at last succeeded in asserting himself, partly through the habit of authority, and partly because the brothers had shouted themselves breathless.

'One moment, Martin. I will call you so, because I have known you a long time, and your father too. I understand your anger at the things Haviland has said. They were unpardonable, as I am sure he will realise when he comes to his right mind. But you must remember that he has been greatly shocked and upset – as we all have been – by this very very painful business. And it is not fair to say that Haviland has tried to "do you out" of anything. He knew nothing about this iniquitous will, and he naturally saw to it that the funeral arrangements were carried out in the usual way. You must settle the future amicably between you, just as you would have done had the will not been accidentally mislaid. Now, Martin – and Haviland too – think it over. My dear boys, this scene is simply appalling. It really must not happen. Surely the estate can be divided up in a friendly manner between you. It is horrible that an old man's body should be a bone of contention between his own sons, just over a matter of money.'

'I'm sorry,' said Martin. 'I forgot myself. You're quite right, sir. Look here, Haviland, forget it. I'll let you have half the money—'

'Half the money! But it's all mine. *You'll* let me have half? How damned generous! My own money!'

'No, old man. It's mine at the moment. The governor's not buried yet, you know. That's right, isn't it, Mr Frobisher-Pym?'

'Yes; the money is yours, legally, at this moment. You must see that, Haviland. But your brother offers you half, and—'

'Half! I'm damned if I'll take half. The man's tried to swindle me out of it. I'll send for the police, and have him put in gaol for robbing the Church. You see if I don't. Give me the telephone.'

'Excuse me,' said Wimsey. 'I don't want to butt in on your

family affairs any more than I have already, but I really don't advise you to send for the police.'

'*You* don't, eh? What the hell's it got to do with you?'

'Well,' said Wimsey deprecatingly, 'if this will business comes into court, I shall probably have to give evidence, because I was the bird who found the thing, don't you see?'

'Well, then?'

'Well, then. They might ask how long the will was supposed to have been where I found it.'

Haviland appeared to swallow something which obstructed his speech.

'What about it, curse you!'

'Yes. Well, you see, it's rather odd when you come to think of it. I mean, your late father must have hidden that will in the bookcase before he went abroad. That was – how long ago? Three years? Five years?'

'About four years.'

'Quite. And since then your bright caretaker has let the damp get into the library, hasn't she? No fires, and the window getting broken, and so on. Ruinous to the books. Very distressin' to anybody like myself, you know. Yes. Well, supposin' they asked that question about the will – and you said it had been there in the damp for four years. Wouldn't they think it a bit funny if I told 'em that there was a big damp stain like a grinning face on the end of the bookshelf, and a big, damp, grinning face on the jolly old *Nüremberg Chronicle* to correspond with it, and no stain on the will which had been sittin' for four years between the two?'

Mrs Haviland screamed suddenly. 'Haviland! You fool! You utter fool!'

'Shut up!'

Haviland snapped round at his wife with a cry of rage, and she collapsed into a chair, with her hand snatched to her mouth.

'Thank you, Winnie,' said Martin. 'No, Haviland – don't trouble to explain. Winnie's given the show away. So you knew – you *knew* about the will, and you deliberately hid it away and let the funeral go on. I'm immensely obliged to you – nearly as obliged as I am to the discreet Graham. Is it fraud or conspiracy or what, to conceal wills? Mr Frobisher-Pym will know.'

'Dear, dear!' said the magistrate. 'Are you certain of your facts, Wimsey?'

'Positive,' said Wimsey, producing the *Nüremberg Chronicle* from under his arm. 'Here's the stain – you can see it yourself. Forgive me for having borrowed your property, Mr Burdock. I was rather afraid Mr Haviland might think this little discrepancy over in the still watches of the night, and decide to sell the *Chronicle*, or give it away, or even think it looked better without its back pages and cover. Allow me to return it to you, Mr Martin – intact. You will perhaps excuse my saying that I don't very much admire any of the rôles in this melodrama. It throws, as Mr Pecksniff would say, a sad light on human nature. But I resent extremely the way in which I was wangled up to that bookshelf and made to be the bright little independent witness who found the will. I may be an ass, Mr Haviland Burdock, but I'm not a bloody ass. Good night. I will wait in the car till you are all ready.'

Wimsey stalked out with some dignity.

Presently he was followed by the vicar and by Mr Frobisher-Pym.

'Mortimer's taking Haviland and his wife to the station,' said the magistrate. 'They're going back to town at once. You can send their traps off in the morning, Hancock. We'd better make ourselves scarce.'

Wimsey pressed the self-starter.

As he did so, a man ran hastily down the steps and came up to him. It was Martin.

'I say,' he muttered. 'You've done me a good turn – more than I deserve, I'm afraid. You must think I'm a damned swine. But I'll see the old man decently put away, and I'll share with Haviland. You mustn't judge him too hardly, either. That wife of his is an awful woman. Run him over head and ears in debt. Bust up his business. I'll see it's all squared up. See? Don't want you to think us too awful.'

'Oh, right-ho!' said Wimsey.

He slipped in the clutch, and faded away into the wet, white fog.

The Motive

G. D. H. and M. Cole

'Murder! Police! Help! Ow! Ai! Oy! Help! Police! Murder!!'
Even at seven o'clock of a cold and dark December morning
the raucous voice of the maid from No. 10, screaming as
urgently as a train whistle at the front entrance to Mimosa
Mansions, quickly collected a crowd in the dingy Fulham
street.

'Cripes, what's that awful row?' said the grocer at the
corner to the grocer's wife, who was just giving him a cup of
tea before he got up.

'That! That's old Mrs Wansberbeck's Emily, from ten
Mimosa. I'd know 'er great foghorn beller anywhere,' said
his wife. 'An' there mustn't 'arf be a shindy on, jedging by
the 'owl she's makin'. Not one to lift 'er tongue for nothing,
Emily ain't. An' if you were 'arf a man you'd pull on yer
pants and look around to see wot's up, and me with me 'ands
full getting yer breakfast and the fire an' all!'

But long before the grocer, or indeed more than a tithe of the interested neighbours, could pull their pants on and get to the spot, PC Hawkes, with a 'Now, what's all this noise about?' had shouldered his way through the knot at the door, and had gripped by her upper arms the grim-featured woman, in apron and curlers, who was still shrieking in regular rhythm, albeit rather more hoarsely and with rather less violence.

'Now, then, Mrs Battle,' the constable said again. 'What's all this about?'

'The mistress! Mrs Wansberbeck! She's been murdered! And I know who done it too – the lying, wasting rascal!'

'Sh-sh. Come, come,' said the constable. 'No use shouting like that on the step. You come along with me and we'll just 'ave a look. May be some mistake about it, you know.'

But as soon as Emily Battle had taken him up to the first-floor flat, and shown him the bedroom in which her mistress lay, he saw at once that there was no mistake.

As there was no telephone in the flat – he recollected having heard that Mrs Wansberbeck was not one to waste her money on what she regarded as a wanton modern plague – he blew a shrill blast to summon assistance and send his colleague to communicate with headquarters.

'Well, *that* looks plain sailing enough for you,' the police-surgeon said a little while later, as he rose to his feet after an examination of the body. 'Cause of death, heart failure following attempted strangulation. There are the marks of thumbs on her windpipe, but she wasn't in fact strangled. Her heart gave out first. Time of death, six to eight hours ago – probably round about midnight. Do you a P.M. if you like; but I don't suppose we'll get much more out of it.'

'That means murder,' said the Divisional Inspector, Garfield by name.

'Well, I should say so. Your man might put up a plea of accident or manslaughter, seeing that she didn't actually die of strangulation. Say he tried to give her a fright or something. But I shouldn't think that was likely to wash, with the old girl in her nightgown, and his fingers on her throat and all. Well, so long. Let me know if you want anything more of me.'

'Marks of his fingers on her throat,' the Divisional Inspector murmured to himself. 'Ah! And the question is, whose fingers are they? Hawkes!'

'Yessir.'

'Didn't you say there was a woman here who said she knew who'd done it?'

'Yessir. Emily Battle, sir. Deceased's factotum, sir.'

'We'll have her in here. Stop a minute, Hawkes – this is on your beat, isn't it? Anything you can tell me about this outfit, first?'

PC Hawkes had not very much to tell. The dead woman he knew only slightly. She was reported to be a terror and very rich – also a miser, or she would not have lived in Mimosa Mansions, where the flats were of the £100-a-year order. 'It wasn't robbery, though,' Inspector Garfield commented. 'There's not a sign of anything having been ransacked here. At least, if it was robbery it was robbery by someone who knew very well where to find what he wanted.' She had never troubled the police in any way, though Hawkes understood she was a terrible trial to the landlord. She had not many visitors; there was a relation – nephew, he believed – who came along every so often. And now and then she had a friend in. What she did with her time he didn't know. As to the servant, Emily Battle, she was a holy one with her tongue and no mistake. As ugly as sin and the terror of the tradespeople. But so far as he knew she was fond enough of the old lady; anyway, she'd been with her for donkey's years.

'Strong?' asked Garfield.

'As a horse, sir.'

'Um. Not that it was needed,' Garfield said. He was thinking of the possible temptations of an annuity to a servant who had lived many years with a mistress who was a terror and a miser. And at present the murder had all the appearance of being an inside job. 'Got to get a look at her will – if there is one,' he made a mental note. 'All right, Hawkes, in with her.'

But a very few words with Emily Battle were sufficient to dissipate any suspicion of her guilt. She was certainly ugly, and she was certainly not sweet-tempered. But no servant who had just murdered her mistress, the inspector felt, could have feigned her purple, swollen face, her hot floods of tears, or the shrieks of rage with which she demanded that the police should stop wasting time over her and immediately arrest the murderer. For Emily Battle, as she had told the constable, knew who the murderer was.

And who was he?

Why, that lying, ungrateful, dirty, swindling nephew of her dear mistress, that – that *beast*, that viper for whom she had done everything in the world that anybody could, while he—

Yes, but who *was* he?

Franklin Stanhope, his *name* was (as if that was the least important thing about him). And he was her own sister's son, and he—

Yes, but why was she so sure that he had murdered his aunt?

At this Emily Battle broke into a long and loud tirade, so interspersed with sobs and abuse of the police that it was difficult to make out for some time what she was saying. Reduced to some sort of order, the main chapters of her story appeared to run somewhat as follows:

(1) That Franklin Stanhope, the son of Mrs Wansberbeck's sister, and, so far as Emily knew, her only living relative, was heir to Mrs Wansberbeck's money, which must be a considerable amount, though Emily did not know how much, because the old lady had told her that she did not spend above the half of the interest on her investments. No (in reply to a question), she didn't keep money about the place; she thought it was a fool's trick. She put it all in the bank the minute she got it.

(2) That Franklin Stanhope was a barrister, but a barrister who never did any work, so far as Emily knew, but played around in night-clubs and at race-courses, borrowed money on his expectations, and was always coming to his aunt for financial assistance. That up till a few years ago she had paid practically without demur; but since then she had got more and more angry with his sponging and fecklessness, and had talked more than once about the possibility of changing her will and leaving all her money to the Cats' Home.

(3) That on the previous evening Franklin Stanhope had

come to see his aunt, and they had had a fearful row. Emily had not let him in herself, as it had been her afternoon out, and she had left Mrs Wansberbeck's tea and supper ready for her; but when she came in about half-past nine (for she wasn't one who held with all those late nights) she had seen Mr Franklin's hat in the hall and heard them going at it hammer and tongs in the living room. She had looked in to see whether Mrs Wansberbeck wanted anything, and had been roughly told to hold her tongue and get out. So she had gone to bed, but the row had continued; and it was not until she had been in bed some time – between half-past ten and eleven, she judged – that she had heard Mr Franklin go out of the flat and bang the door, and Mrs Wansberbeck, a few minutes afterwards, come out of the sitting-room and go into the bathroom.

'But, stop a moment,' Garfield said at this point.

'You say you heard your mistress go into the bathroom *after* you heard the front door bang?' Emily Battle nodded. 'But, then, that means she was alive when Mr Stanhope left her last night.'

'Maybe,' said Emily. 'But what's to prevent him coming back in the dead of night, when we was all asleep, and doing 'er in? He'd got his own key to the flat, and that outer door ain't never locked.'

'But isn't there a bolt or anything to this front door?'

'Maybe,' said Emily. '*But how if it wasn't bolted?* How if my mistress, being a bit forgetful as she was sometimes when she was upset like, and worrying over that young waster, hadn't remembered to bolt the door after him? Anyhow, it wasn't fastened when I went down to take the milk in this morning, and you can put that in your pipe and smoke it, Mr Whatever-your-name-is!'

'Oh!' said the inspector. 'You're sure of that?'

'Take my oath on it, if it wasn't against my principles to swear.'

'Very well. I don't think I need keep you any longer, Mrs Battle. What is the address of this Franklin Stanhope?'

'Twenty-three, Jermyn Court – and I hope it burns down on him!' said Emily Battle.

'Umph!' said Inspector Garfield to his subordinates at large. 'Looks a bit awkward for the young fellow, if what the wench says is true. Anyway, it'll be fairly easy to check up on. Rogers, you go and ring up Jermyn Court, and see if his high-and-mightiness is receiving visitors; and, by the way, you might find out whether that maid knows who were Mrs Wansberbeck's lawyers. I forgot to ask her. I'm going to get the Yard onto it right away; it's more their affair than ours – still, we might as well get what information we can ready for them.'

The Yard works quickly, and Garfield's subordinate, who was anxious for promotion, worked quickly too, so that before the afternoon was far advanced information had been sought and secured from various quarters. It had not been possible to interview Mr Franklin Stanhope, for his chambers in Jermyn Court said that he was not at home, had not been home during the previous night, though he was expected back any minute. Nor had Mrs Wansberbeck's lawyer, Mr Jeffrey Neeliwit, been found, for he was in Norfolk on business and would not be back until the following day; but Mrs

Wansberbeck's bank manager had agreed, albeit in guarded language, that Mrs Wansberbeck's account was in very good health, and might even turn out to be larger than anyone had expected. And rapid, but careful, inquiries amongst those who were likely to know had disclosed that Franklin Stanhope's financial position was quite as parlous as his aunt's maid had indicated. He had spent and borrowed right and left, and some of those who had advanced him money on his expectations, as well as his ordinary creditors, were beginning to press him hard for repayment. In fact, it looked as though he were in a bad way.

So it happened that, a little while after the clock on St. James's had struck eight, William Speed, a young Scotland Yard inspector, very anxious to do himself credit on his first murder case, but very bored and cold after a long vigil outside Jermyn Court, received the signal from the local man that his bird had returned, and after a second long and more irritating delay was ushered into the presence of Franklin Stanhope.

Speed tried to put into practice the psychological instructions he had received at the Police College, and to sum up his man at sight. The most obvious thing about Franklin Stanhope was that he was in a very bad temper: the second that he had had a very thorough night-out on the previous evening, and that he had been trying to repair the effects of it in the usual way. He was not drunk; but he was not far from it, and he had certainly reached the quarrelsome stage. For the rest, he was a big fellow, older than Speed had somehow expected to find him, good-looking, probably, when he was in better physical condition, and with a face that was not totally devoid of intelligence or attraction, though he was not out to attract at the moment. For primarily he was cross.

'Well, what do *you* want?' he asked in a voice that was more like a snarl than anything else, making no move either to rise or to offer his visitor a chair.

'I want a few words with you, sir,' Speed said, taking the chair that was not offered.

'What about?'

'About your aunt, Mrs Wansberbeck.'

'*What* about my aunt?' Stanhope glared at him.

'I don't know whether you have heard, sir, that your aunt died very suddenly last night?'

'Heard! Of course I've heard! What are the evening papers for, do you suppose? It's all splashed over the front pages. And what d'you mean by saying "Died very suddenly"! She was murdered, wasn't she? You don't have to break it to me. Good God, I've been breaking it to myself all the afternoon!' said Stanhope with an ugly guffaw.

'I'm sorry, sir—'

'Sorry be damned. You haven't come here to tell me you're sorry. What *have* you come here for, that's what I want to know. Out with it! But it's no use asking me to tell you anything about my aunt's death, because I don't know anything.'

'Excuse me, sir,' said Speed, as politely as he could, 'but you being the last person to see her alive, and you also being her heir—'

He got no further, for he was interrupted by a vast and hysterical peal of laughter from Stanhope, who slapped the table and roared at his joke.

'Ha! ha! ha! ha! Her *heir* – that's a good one, that is! Ho!

ho! That's one of the best I've ever heard! You found out I
was her heir, did you, and you've come toddling round with
your mouth full of butter to see how I'd take her death, and
to arrest me for murder if I wasn't in mourning! Well, I'm
not in mourning, and I'm not going into mourning for her
either – damned skinflinty old bitch—'

'Mr Stanhope,' Speed interrupted, 'it is my duty to warn
you—'

'Warn away, my bright boy. You'll laugh on the other side
of your mouth in a minute. Now listen. I *was* her heir, as you
found out, you clever little lad, you; *but I'm not her heir any
longer*. Yesterday – just yesterday, mark you – my dear aunt
made a new will and cut me off with five quid and her bless-
ing. So what do you make of that, my good Nosey Parker?
Pretty joke, isn't it? Ha! ha! ha! You know, if you could see
your own face you'd laugh yourself.'

'Do I understand you to say, sir—'

'You understand me to say that my aunt disinherited me
yesterday. Made a new will and left all her money to the Cats'
Home. She told me so herself. And then goes and gets herself
killed before I've had time to do anything about it! ... Look
here,' said Stanhope, pouring himself a large whisky and
gulping it down, 'I've told you all I know, and I don't like
the look of your face. I didn't do your murder: I haven't any
motive, and if you want an alibi, I was drinking in the Pink
Ox from the moment I left her last night until God knows
what time, and there's lashings of fellows will tell you so. So
suppose you try pushing off.'

*

'I didn't see what else I could do, sir,' said Inspector Speed, reporting rather crestfallen to his chief at Scotland Yard. 'The man was very offensive; but he was three parts drunk, and if his story was true he must have had the dickens of a shock, both last night, when he found he was disinherited, and this afternoon, when he found the old lady had died with the new will unaltered. I couldn't blame him, at that, for cutting up rough. Of course, I know he might have killed her in a passion, like the doctor said, not meaning to do it but just giving her a shake so that she popped off. But, though he might likely have done that at once, as soon as ever she'd told him, I didn't somehow see his going away and coming back to do it. And he was very confident about his alibi afterwards – just chucked it at me as though there wasn't any doubt it would hold water. So I didn't see what I could do but come away, sir; though looking back now it seems to me I may have been wrong.'

'I think you acted quite correctly, Speed,' Superintendent Wilson said to him with a kindly smile. 'What's more, I think you're justified already; for things have been happening while you've been out, and we've been round the place and investigated things a little more thoroughly than the local people did – of course, this morning they thought they'd got their bird on toast. For instance – this Franklin Stanhope, what sort of sized man is he?'

'Oh, a big chap. Five foot ten at least – maybe a bit more. I didn't see him standing up,' Speed said. 'And broad-shouldered and all. Strong as a horse.'

'Hands? Did you notice them at all?'

'Big, like the rest of him. Broader than mine, I'd say,' said Speed, spreading his own out. 'Great flat thumbs.'

'So I should suppose. Well, the doctor's had a close look at the lady's neck and *he* says for certain that the marks on it were made either by a quite small man or a woman. That alone looks like letting our friend out, for it's not very likely that he would have had an accomplice. But there's another thing. When we came to go round the room carefully, we found the print of a dusty shoe on the linoleum – a man's shoe, size six about, on the edge of the linoleum pointing towards the wardrobe. And, Speed, *inside* that wardrobe we found traces of dusty feet – not quite clear, but pretty certainly the same sized foot, made by somebody standing inside the wardrobe. What do you make of that?'

'You mean – her murderer was standing *inside* the wardrobe, waiting for her to go to bed?'

'Looks like it.'

'But he couldn't! He'd suffocate, standing there any length of time.'

'I'm not so sure about that. The wardrobe's a great big piece of furniture, with a good many cracks and not many clothes in it. If he opened the door a chink when she wasn't in the room he'd get plenty of air. And we don't know how long he had to stand there.'

'But how on earth did he get in – I mean into the flat at all?'

'That's a mystery,' Wilson said. 'The maid swears she let nobody in, and one can hardly imagine that Mrs Wansberbeck herself let her murderer into the flat and put him away quietly in a wardrobe to suit his convenience. And there's no other way in.'

'What about the windows?'

'He wouldn't have to be merely a small man, he'd have to be a squirrel, to get in at those windows,' Wilson said. 'There's no way of climbing up, and the windows are all screwed down with patent screws that leave about three inches open at the top.'

'Perhaps,' said Speed, 'he came while the maid was out, pretending to sell vacuums or collect for something, and Mrs Wansberbeck let him in herself?'

'And then put him in the wardrobe? Besides,' said Wilson, 'Emily Battle said Mrs Wansberbeck would never do anything of the sort. She loathed travellers and collectors of every sort, and always put the door on the chain, when she was by herself, before answering it; and if they were collecting, slammed it in their faces. The police sports fund,' he added with a chuckle, 'bears her out in that, and one of them told me he'd been there when a little chap came about some charity or other – I'm not sure that it wasn't actually the Cats' Home – and was really shocked by the way she treated him ... But besides – who on earth *was* the fellow?'

'Was it the servant, perhaps?' Speed, very much flattered at receiving the confidence of his superior, suggested. 'You said it might have been a woman as well as a small man. And maybe she was left something in the will. Or what about whoever inherited if Stanhope didn't finding out about it and killing her quick before she'd time to alter her mind? I don't suppose she really left it to the Cats' Home.'

'I don't suppose she did,' Wilson agreed. 'But it must have been very quick work, mustn't it? However, I quite agree that the next thing to look at is the will, and I'm hoping Mr Neeliwit will turn up tomorrow and provide us with some useful information. I must confess I don't quite like the idea of Emily Battle as a suspect. For one thing, her feet are much too big, and anyway it's not really likely to have been a woman. The shoes were pretty certainly a man's.'

But Mr Neeliwit, when he came, provided no helpful information at all. He confirmed the existence of the new will, and stated that he had received an urgent letter from Mrs Wansberbeck, on the morning before her death, demanding that he should wait on her that afternoon with a new will, on lines which she laid down for him, all ready for her to sign. He duly came, and was admitted by Mrs Wansberbeck herself (which explained why Emily had not mentioned it) and then and there she signed the will, giving, as the reason for her haste, that her nephew was coming to see her that evening and she wanted to have a nice surprise for him. She had then given back the will, which Mr Neeliwit now produced, and Wilson eagerly opened, only to lay it down with a gasp of disgust. For the bulk – indeed, almost the whole – of Mrs Wansberbeck's considerable fortune was indeed and in so many words devised to the Royal Victoria Cats' Home, in Fulham. If Mr Neeliwit had not been a lawyer of the greatest correctness he would have been put to it not to laugh at Wilson's face.

It was comic, perhaps; but it was also extremely annoying. For there was nothing in that will from end to end to suggest a motive for murder. There was fifty pounds (not five) to Franklin Stanhope; but fifty pounds would have been a drop in the bucket of his liabilities. There were a few, a very few, odd legacies, mostly to institutions; and to Emily Battle there was another fifty pounds, the furniture, and the remainder of the lease of Mrs Wansberbeck's flat ('That's about four months,' the lawyer interjected. 'She had it on a six-monthly tenancy'). Otherwise there was nothing – nothing whatever to show who was the little man who had stood concealed in Mrs Wansberbeck's cupboard, and why he should have wanted to murder Mrs Wansberbeck. 'You saw the will signed yourself, I suppose?' asked Wilson as a last resort. Mr Neeliwit said indeed he did, and witnessed as well. He pointed to the signatures of the witnesses, Dorothy Markins and Edward Cockburn, and added, in the tone of one supplying unnecessary information to fools, that he had no idea who they were. Mrs Wansberbeck just produced them – out of a wardrobe, maybe.

And there the matter stood. Weeks went by and there was no light on the Fulham murder. Nobody came forward who had ever heard Mrs Wansberbeck speak of a little man, or even seen a little man anywhere near her flat; nobody turned up who had even the ghost of a reason for murdering her. The case was relegated to the file of genuinely unsolved mysteries; and nobody except Wilson, who could not but feel that there must be *some* clue which he could have found if he had been more wide-awake, gave it another thought.

At last, however, nearly four months after the murder, he heard that a Mrs Battle was asking for him, who, when she was admitted, proved to be Emily, as tough and as truculent as ever, and brandishing a very dirty white pocket-handkerchief.

'If you've not forgotten all about my poor mistress,' she began without ceremony, 'I thought you might be interested in this. I was a-clearing out 'er things, poor dear, prior to moving out of the place, and *this* is what I found, right down at the back of the wardrobe, where you people said 'e was 'iding, and where no man's handkerchief ought to be and that I do know!'

'Most probably Mr Stanhope's,' said Wilson, glancing at it without much interest.

'That it never! Mr Franklin never 'ad one o' them toora-looral things like this. Silk's the cheapest that's good enough for me lord. 'Owever, if you don't want it you needn't. I jest thought you coppers might be able to find out oos it was.'

'We'll try, anyway,' Wilson said. 'I see there's been a laundry-mark on it some time.'

'*And* a faldida kind of initial,' Emily said.

'Anyhow, thank you very much for bringing it along, and I trust we may get something out of it. Good morning, Mrs Battle.'

Without much hope, Wilson set the machinery of Scotland Yard in motion to trace the dirty handkerchief. Once before, he knew, a murderer had been tracked down through a laundry-mark; but that was probably a fluke. However, when, ten days later, some information came in, after one perusal he lifted his head like a dog snuffing a trail, and sent for *Whitaker's Almanack*. For a few moments he searched it, and then took up his hat and went purposefully out. He was about to make a long shot – but first he needed some more information. He sought out Mrs Emily Battle and asked her, 'Do you know who either Dorothy Markins or Edward Cockburn is?'

'Mrs Markins has the flat below ours – and a proper piece

of goods she is too,' said Emily promptly. 'T'other's nobody *I* ever 'eard of.'

'Thank you,' said Wilson, and departed to call on the flat below, luckily finding its mistress at home.

Of Mrs Markins, whom he found washing her hair and eating chocolates, he asked only one thing, that she should cast her mind back to the day of the signing of Mrs Wansberbeck's will, and see if she could tell him anything about her co-witness.

'Why, that I can't,' Mrs Markins replied frankly. 'I'd never set eyes on him before, and what's more, I don't believe Mrs Wansberbeck had either. You see, it was like this. She came down to me, and asked if me and my husband would come up and sign something for her. But my husband was out and she was right put about, saying she was in a great hurry for it; so we went out to see if we couldn't find anyone. And there was this funny little fellow on the stairs going up – not five-foot high, he wasn't. I think he was begging or collecting, myself; but Mrs Wansberbeck never took any notice. 'Here,' she says, 'you'll do. Come on.' And in she hustled him, without a by-your-leave or with-your-leave.'

'I see. And,' said Wilson, 'did Mrs Wansberbeck, while you were there, say anything to either of you about the document you were witnessing?'

'That she did,' Mrs Markins giggled. 'Told us all about it, and at the top of her voice, she was so pleased with herself. Proper old devil she was, if you'll pardon me.'

'Thank you very much indeed,' said Wilson; and with the hastiest of leave-takings he hurried off. He was very anxious indeed to interview a grey little man who lived in a grey office in Fulham. When he left that office his case was finished.

'I killed her,' the document ran. 'It seemed like the hand of God. She was a rich hard woman, and she had no use for her money, and she would never give me a penny for my poor cats, she slammed the door in my face. Old rich women are like that. I thought I would try just once more to move her heart, for we had no money and the trustees were going to close down and throw my poor cats on the street. And then she met me on the stairs and took me and made me witness her will leaving us all her money – but it was no use unless she died soon. And I might never have got in again, because they kept the door on the chain. So when she said you can go, I didn't go; I let the woman go, and then I went into her bedroom and hid in the wardrobe. I waited till she'd gone to bed and then I came out and killed her, and the door wasn't bolted, so I went home quietly.

'There wasn't any reason she should live; she was a hard, mean old woman, and her money wasn't any good till she was dead. And I know you can't benefit by the result of a crime, or witness a will that leaves you anything; but I'm not a trustee of the Home, I'm only a salaried employee and can't benefit at all, so the cats will be all right whatever happens to me. I thought of all that before I did it.

'(Signed) CECIL EDWARD COCKBURN,
'*Superintendent*,
'*Royal Victoria Cats' Home.*'
'They won't hang him,' said Wilson. 'But I wish the law allowed life sentences to be served in a cats' home.'

Underneath the Mistletoe Last Night

Mark Billingham

Jack knew all about 'being good for goodness sake', he'd heard it in that song, but he didn't think opening his presents a few hours early would count as being bad. Besides, he had been asleep and even if it was still dark outside, it was already Christmas Day, so it wasn't really cheating, was it?

He lay awake a few minutes longer, wondering if it was snowing outside; if Rudolph shared that carrot they had left for him with all the other reindeer; and if the elves were already working on the toys for next year. He tried thinking about all sorts of things, but he couldn't keep his mind off those shiny parcels under the tree downstairs.

He climbed out of bed. He decided that bare feet would be quieter, so ignoring the Sam-7 slippers at the foot of his bed, he crept slowly out of his room and downstairs. He took one

141

step at a time, wincing at every creak. The door to the living room was open, so he could see the tree before he reached the bottom of the stairs.

What was lying underneath it. Who …

The red of his coat and the white of his thick beard. The shiny black belt and boots. Not as fat as Jack had been expecting, but maybe he was on a diet.

He waited for a minute at the foot of the stairs, then padded softly into the living room. He had always thought it must be very tiring. All those houses to visit in one night. If Father Christmas chose this particular house to have a nap in, did that mean other children would not be getting their presents? Or was this the last house on his journey?

Jack crept a little closer, then stopped. He let out a small gasp and clamped a hand across his mouth. He watched and waited for the chest to move, to hear a breath or a snuffle, but he could hear nothing but the low hum of the fridge in the kitchen and a strange hiss inside in his own head.

One arm was lying funny. A boot was half off his foot.

A different sort of red, where it shouldn't have been.

The boy turned and bolted up the stairs. He charged into his parents' room, shouting for his mum. She sat up and blinked and he ran to her, breathless, fighting to get the words out.

'Somebody killed Father Christmas …'

Tom Thorne had not needed to think very long before signing himself up for the Christmas Day shift. It made no real difference to him. There was no family to spend it with and, as far as he was concerned, Christmas Day was as good or bad a day to die as any other.

None of his regular team was at the house when he arrived, and clambering into the plastic bodysuit in the small front garden, he exchanged cursory nods of recognition or understanding with those officers already there.

We're the sad buggers. The ones with no lives.

Through a gaggle of SOCOs and police photographers, he was relieved to see the familiar figure of Phil Hendricks crouched over the body. The pathologist had been dumped by his partner a few weeks previously and he and Thorne had already agreed to have Christmas lunch together at a local pub if no calls came in. Now, it looked like they would have to settle for turkey sandwiches and a few beers at Thorne's flat.

'This is a strange one,' Hendricks said.

Thorne thought, 'They're the ones I like best', but just nodded.

'Who the hell would want to do Santa in?' The pathologist laid a gloved finger against the dead man's face. 'The tooth fairy? Jack Frost ...?'

'I'm keeping an open mind,' Thorne said. 'What are we looking at?'

'Single stab wound, far as I can see.'

'Knife?'

A DC Thorne did not know appeared behind him. 'No sign of it,' he said. He nodded back towards the kitchen. 'Broken window at the back and sod all under the tree except our friend here. Pretty obvious he disturbed a burglar ...'

Thorne had to concede that it looked that way. Easy

pickings for thieves on Christmas Eve. People out celebrating and a healthy selection of must-have gadgets sitting under trees in nine out of ten living rooms. 'Where's the wife?' he asked.

'Upstairs,' the DC said. 'Family Liaison Officer's with her.'

'What about the boy?'

'A car's taking him to his mum's parents.'

Thorne nodded.

'By all accounts the kid didn't get a good look, so he doesn't know … you know. Not yet, anyway.'

Thorne watched as the funeral directors came into the room. They unzipped the body bag and knelt beside the dead man, which Thorne took as his cue to go upstairs and meet the widow.

Wendy Fielding sat on the edge of the bed, a female Family Liaison Officer next to her. Each cradled a mug of tea. Always tea, Thorne thought, wondering why the Murder Squad was not looking towards Tetley for some sort of sponsorship. He told the FLO to step outside, asked Mrs Fielding if she felt up to talking. She nodded and Thorne sat down on a large wooden trunk against the wall.

'I'm sorry for your loss,' he said. The room was dimly lit by a bedside lamp, but the first milky slivers of morning light were creeping through a gap in the curtains.

She said, 'Thank you' and tried to smile. She was in her late thirties, Thorne guessed, though for obvious reasons she looked a little older. She wore a powder-blue housecoat, but when she shifted on the bed, Thorne could see that the front of the pale nightdress beneath was soaked with blood.

'Can you take me through what happened this morning?' Thorne asked.

She nodded without raising her head and took a deep breath. 'It was just after one o'clock,' she said. 'I know because I looked at the clock when Jack came in.' She spoke quietly and quickly, as though worried that, were she to hesitate even for a second, she might fall apart. 'He told me that Father Christmas was dead ... that someone had killed him in the living room. I told him to stay here ... I tucked him up in bed and ...' Then there was hesitation, and Thorne watched her swallow hard. She looked up at him. 'He doesn't know it's his dad. He still believes in ...' She puffed out her cheeks, swallowed again. 'When do you think I should tell him?'

'We'll put you in touch with bereavement counsellors,' Thorne told her. 'They'll be able to advise you.'

'Right,' she said.

Thorne thought he could smell booze on her, but said nothing. He could hardly blame the woman for needing a stiff drink to go with her tea.

'Tell me about the Santa outfit,' he said.

Another attempt at a smile. 'Alan had been planning it for ages,' she said. 'It was his office party last night and they always have a Father Christmas, so he decided he was going to bring the costume home then dress up in it to take Jack's presents up. He pretends to be asleep, you know? You have kids?'

Thorne shook his head.

'Alan thought it would be special, you know? If Jack saw Father Christmas putting the presents at the end of his bed.'

'So you went downstairs?'

'He was just lying there, like Jack said he was. I knelt down and picked him up, but I knew he'd gone. There was so much blood on his chest and coming out of his mouth … sorry.'

'Take a minute,' Thorne said.

'It's fine. I'm fine.'

'Did you hear anything before that?' Thorne asked. 'The glass in the back door breaking? Somebody moving about downstairs?'

'I'm a heavy sleeper,' she said. 'I was dead to the world until Jack came in.'

Thorne nodded, wondering if the alcohol he could smell had actually been drunk the night before.

'So, you think they were in the house when Alan came home?'

'We're still working downstairs,' Thorne said. 'But if he disturbed a burglar that would mean he was already wearing the costume, which seems a bit odd.'

'Maybe he changed into it at the party.'

'Maybe,' Thorne said.

They both turned at the soft knock and turned to see the Detective Constable standing awkwardly in the doorway.

'Something you need to see,' he said.

Thorne got down on his belly to peer beneath the tree and saw a mobile phone sitting hard against the skirting board.

He gave the officer the nod and the man crawled under the tree, his plastic bodysuit snagging on the branches as he stretched to reach the phone. Having retrieved the handset, he handed it across to Thorne, who almost dropped it when it began to ring in his hand. Everyone in the room froze.

'Write the number down,' he barked.

The DC scrabbled for pen and notebook and scribbled down the number on the phone's display. They waited for the phone to stop ringing, then heard the alert that told them a message had been left.

'Shall we?' Thorne asked.

The DC held his notebook out so that Thorne could read the number and Thorne dialled.

A woman answered. She said, 'Hello,' and when Thorne began to introduce himself, she hung up.

'Get on to the phone company,' Thorne said.

'Our burglar dropped his phone, you reckon?' Hendricks asked. 'Looks like you might have got yourself an early Christmas present.'

'I was hoping for an iPad,' Thorne said.

Bright and early on a freezing Boxing day and Thorne was standing in a Forensic Science Service lab next to a balding technician named Turnbull. Thorne knew the man was recently divorced. Another sad case who preferred working to sitting at home alone and wondering if his kids were having a good day.

'What have we got?'

'Two text messages,' Turnbull said, pointing to the phone. '7.37 on Christmas Eve and again half an hour later. Plus the voice message that was left when you were at the murder scene.'

Thorne had already established when Alan Fielding had left home to go to his firm's Christmas party. One message had been sent just before he left and the second would have arrived when he was on his way there.

'Let's see,' Thorne said.

Turnbull handed him a transcript of the messages.

19.37. 24/12/11. It's me. Just wondered if you'd left yet. I'm guessing ur having trouble getting away. Can't wait to see u. x

Then …

19.54. 24/12/11. Hope ur on your way. Hurry up and get here will u? Can't wait to give u yr Xmas present. I know ur going to like it. x

And last, a transcript of the voice message, left in the early hours of Christmas morning.

'Just me. Couldn't sleep. Tonight was amazing though. I know you can't tell her today … I'm not expecting you to, but do it soon, OK? Oh, and you're the sexiest Santa I've ever seen …'

'So, what do you think?' Turnbull asked.

Thorne stared at the phone. He already knew who the messages were from. The same woman who had called the phone found underneath the Christmas tree; the phone they thought had been left by whoever had killed Alan Fielding. Thorne now knew that the phone was Fielding's, that he had forgotten to take it with him, and that the caller was Angela Massey, a twenty-four-year-old secretary who worked at the same company as he did.

Thorne had spoken to her on Christmas Day, just before the umpteenth repeat of *The Great Escape*. He was due to interview her formally later that day.

He blinked slowly. His head was still thick after the night before, when he and Hendricks had drunk far too much and swapped distinctly unseasonal banter.

'Knife went straight through his heart,' Hendricks had said. 'Probably dead before he hit the deck.'

'Something, I suppose.'

'Not the best way to round off Christmas Eve.'

'Yeah, well …'

'What?'

'I think he'd had quite a good night up to that point.'

'So, that help you?' Turnbull asked. 'The stuff on the phone?'

'Yeah that helps,' Thorne said. 'Helps me screw up Christmas for at least a couple more people.'

'I need to get Jack from my mum's, so can we just get this over with?' Wendy Fielding shifted in her seat, bit down on her bottom lip. 'I haven't told him yet, but he's been asking questions about his dad.' She looked down at the scarred metal tabletop. 'My mum told him that Alan had to go on a business trip …'

'This shouldn't take long,' Thorne said.

Though concessions had been made to the season elsewhere in the station – a few strings of tinsel in the canteen, an ironic sprig of mistletoe in the custody suite – the interview room was as bland and bare as it was for the rest of the year. Thorne turned on the twin CD recorders, pointed to the camera high on the wall to let Wendy Fielding know that their interview was being recorded.

'I don't understand,' she said. 'I thought you just wanted a chat.'

'Where are the presents, Wendy?'

She looked at him. 'How the hell should I know? Thieving bastard sold them for drugs, most likely. That's what they do, isn't it?'

'Some of them,' Thorne said.

'I don't know how they live with themselves.' She shook her head, disgusted, but she would not meet Thorne's eyes.

'You're right, of course,' Thorne said. 'Our burglar would probably have sold your son's Christmas presents for a few wraps of heroin. If he'd existed.'

Now she looked, eyes wide.

'I'm guessing you stashed them up in the loft or somewhere. Along with the knife. That might have been before or after you'd broken the window in the back door. Doesn't really matter.'

'What are you talking about? I think you're the one on drugs ...'

'You really should have thought about the phone though. The one you chucked at your husband. It was the phone that made us think we might catch our burglar, but what was on it told me there wasn't a burglar to catch.' Thorne glanced across, watched the display on the recorder count away the seconds. 'I spoke to Angela Massey yesterday,' he said. 'She's every bit as upset as you were pretending to be.'

'Bitch!' Wendy snapped.

'Not really,' Thorne said. 'Just a girl who was in love with your husband. She claims he was in love with her too.'

'He wouldn't know love if it bit him.'

Thorne nodded. 'It must have killed you,' he said. 'Listening to those messages, knowing he was going to leave. Sitting there getting drunker. Angrier …'

'At Christmas,' she shouted, 'of all the times. What do you imagine that would have done to Jack?'

'What do you think you've done to Jack?'

'I didn't plan it,' she said. She was breathing heavily, desperate suddenly. 'He came back and I confronted him. We argued and all of a sudden I had the kitchen knife. I didn't mean to.'

'You stabbed him through the heart and then went back to bed,' Thorne said. 'You left your husband's body for your six-year-old son to find.'

'I'm a good mother,' she said. 'I don't care what you think. I was clearly no great shakes as a wife, but I'm a damn good mother …'

When Thorne came back into the Incident Room, DS Dave Holland was walking towards him, a broad grin on his face. Singing.

'I saw Mommy killing Santa Claus …'

He saw the look on Thorne's face and stopped.

'Not funny, Dave.'

'Sorry, Guv.' Holland held out a large brown envelope. 'We've had a bit of a whip round,' he said. 'For the boy.'

Thorne took it. Said, 'Thanks.'

'Not the best day to find your dad like that.'

Thorne nodded, having revised his opinion somewhat. Yes, one day was pretty much as good as another to die. But December 25th was a shitty day to lose someone.

Jack Fielding was now staying with Alan Fielding's mother and father. Their claim on the child had been thought that little bit stronger than his maternal grandparents, being as it was the child's mother that had killed their son. Thorne sat awkwardly on their sofa. Drinking tea and eating mince pies, while they did their best to act as if their world hadn't fallen apart.

'What's going to happen to her?' Jack's grandmother asked.

'What do you think?' The old man slurped his tea, pulling a face as though he were drinking hemlock. Perhaps he wished he was.

'She's in Holloway,' Thorne said. 'Likely to be there a while, I should have thought. A big murder trial takes a while to put together and, you know … Christmas and everything.'

'Wasn't easy finding a funeral director either,' the old man said. 'Busy with all the suicides or some such.'

Thorne nodded, thinking, well at least business is booming for somebody.

They said nothing for a while. Thorne stared at the cards on the mantelpiece. The snowmen and reindeer had been replaced by simple white cards with black borders. In deepest sympathy. He glanced at the large, brown envelope on top of the TV.

When Thorne saw the grandmother beam suddenly, he

realised that the boy had come into the room. He turned and saw Jack Fielding hovering in the doorway. He smiled, but the boy looked away.

'Come on, Jack,' the grandmother said. 'Come and say hello.'

The boy took a few steps into the room. A large plastic dinosaur hung from his fingers.

'How are you?' Thorne had probably asked stupider questions, but he could not remember when.

'Where's my mum?' the boy asked.

'She's not very well.'

The boy nodded, as though that made perfect sense. 'Is that because of the dead man?' he asked.

Thorne said that it was.

Jack took another step towards him and leaned against the arm of the sofa. He gently put the toy dinosaur into Thorne's lap. 'It wasn't Father Christmas, was it?'

'No,' Thorne said.

'Was it my daddy?'

Thorne heard the old woman sniff, felt his throat constrict a little. But he kept his eyes fixed on the boy.

'It wasn't Father Christmas,' he said.

Thorne glanced across at the boy's grandmother. Saw something around her eyes and in the small nod of her head. He thought it might mean 'thank you', but he could not be sure.

The New Catacomb

Arthur Conan Doyle

'Look here, Burger,' said Kennedy, 'I do wish that you would confide in me.'

The two famous students of Roman remains sat together in Kennedy's comfortable room overlooking the Corso. The night was cold, and they had both pulled up their chairs to the unsatisfactory Italian stove which threw out a zone of stuffiness rather than of warmth. Outside under the bright winter stars lay the modern Rome, the long, double chain of the electric lamps, the brilliantly lighted cafés, the rushing carriages, and the dense throng upon the footpaths. But inside, in the sumptuous chamber of the rich young English archaeologist, there was only old Rome to be seen. Cracked and timeworn friezes hung upon the walls, grey old busts of senators and soldiers with their fighting heads and their hard, cruel faces peered out from the corners. On the centre table, amidst a litter of inscriptions, fragments and ornaments, there stood the famous reconstruction by Kennedy of the Baths of Caracalla, which excited such interest and admiration when it was exhibited in Berlin. Amphorae hung from the ceiling, and a litter of curiosities strewed the rich red Turkey carpet. And of them all there was not one which was not of the most unimpeachable authenticity, and of the utmost rarity and value; for Kennedy, though little more than thirty, had a European reputation in this particular branch of research, and was, moreover, provided with that long purse which either proves to be a fatal handicap to the student's energies, or, if his mind is still true to its purpose, gives him an enormous advantage in the race for fame. Kennedy had often been seduced by whim and pleasure from his studies, but his mind was an incisive one, capable of long and concentrated efforts which ended in sharp reactions of sensuous languor. His handsome face, with its high, white forehead, its aggressive nose, and its somewhat loose and sensual mouth, was a fair index of the compromise between strength and weakness in his nature.

Of a very different type was his companion, Julius Burger. He came of a curious blend, a German father and an Italian mother, with the robust qualities of the North mingling strangely with the softer graces of the South. Blue Teutonic eyes lightened his sun-browned face, and above them rose a square, massive forehead, with a fringe of close yellow curls lying round it. His strong, firm jaw was clean-shaven, and his companion had frequently remarked how much it suggested those old Roman busts which peered out from the shadows in the corners of his chamber. Under its bluff German strength there lay always a suggestion of

Italian subtlety, but the smile was so honest, and the eyes so frank, that one understood that this was only an indication of his ancestry, with no actual bearing upon his character. In age and in reputation, he was on the same level as his English companion, but his life and his work had both been far more arduous. Twelve years before, he had come as a poor student to Rome, and had lived ever since upon some small endowment for research which had been awarded to him by the University of Bonn. Painfully, slowly, and doggedly, with extraordinary tenacity and single-mindedness, he had climbed from rung to rung of the ladder of fame, until now he was a member of the Berlin Academy, and there was every reason to believe that he would shortly be promoted to the Chair of the greatest of German Universities. But the singleness of purpose which had brought him to the same high level as the rich and brilliant Englishman, had caused him in everything outside their work to stand infinitely below him. He had never found a pause in his studies in which to cultivate the social graces. It was only when he spoke of his own subject that his face was filled with life and soul. At other times he was silent and embarrassed, too conscious of his own limitations in larger subjects, and impatient of that small-talk which is the conventional refuge of those who have no thoughts to express.

And yet for some years there had been an acquaintance-ship which appeared to be slowly ripening into a friendship between these two very different rivals. The base and origin of this lay in the fact that in their own studies each was the only one of the younger men who had knowledge and enthusiasm enough to properly appreciate the other. Their common interests and pursuits had brought them together, and each had been attracted by the other's knowledge. And then gradually something had been added to this. Kennedy had been amused by the frankness and simplicity of his rival, while Burger in turn had been fascinated by the brilliancy and vivacity which had made Kennedy such a favourite in Roman society. I say 'had', because just at the moment the young Englishman was somewhat under a cloud. A love-affair, the details of which had never quite come out, had indicated a heartlessness and callousness upon his part which shocked many of his friends. But in the bachelor circles of students and artists in which he preferred to move there is no very rigid code of honour in such matters, and though a head might be shaken or a pair of shoulders shrugged over the flight of two and the return of one, the general sentiment was probably one of curiosity and perhaps of envy rather than of reprobation.

'Look here, Burger,' said Kennedy, looking hard at the placid face of his companion, 'I do wish that you would confide in me.'

As he spoke he waved his hand in the direction of a rug which lay upon the floor. On the rug stood a long, shallow fruit-basket of the light wicker-work which is used in the Campagna, and this was heaped with a litter of objects, inscribed tiles, broken inscriptions, cracked mosaics, torn papyri, rusty metal ornaments, which to the uninitiated might have seemed to have come straight from a dustman's bin, but which a specialist would have speedily recognised as unique of their kind. The pile of odds and ends in the flat wicker-work basket supplied exactly one of those missing links of social development which are of such interest to the student. It was the German who had brought them in, and the Englishman's eyes were hungry as he looked at them.

'I won't interfere with your treasure-trove, but I should very much like to hear about it,' he continued, while Burger very deliberately lit a cigar. 'It is evidently a discovery of the first importance. These inscriptions will make a sensation throughout Europe.'

'For every one here there are a million there!' said the German. 'There are so many that a dozen savants might spend a lifetime over them, and build up a reputation as solid as the Castle of St Angelo.'

Kennedy sat thinking with his fine forehead wrinkled and his fingers playing with his long, fair moustache.

'You have given yourself away, Burger!' said he at last. 'Your words can only apply to one thing. You have discovered a new catacomb.'

'I had no doubt that you had already come to that conclusion from an examination of these objects.'

'Well, they certainly appeared to indicate it, but your last remarks make it certain. There is no place except a catacomb which could contain so vast a store of relics as you describe.'

'Quite so. There is no mystery about that. I *have* discovered a new catacomb.'

'Where?'

'Ah, that is my secret, my dear Kennedy. Suffice it that it is so situated that there is not one chance in a million of anyone else coming upon it. Its date is different from that of any known catacomb, and it has been reserved for the burial of the highest Christians, so that the remains and the relics are quite different from anything which has ever been seen before. If I was not aware of your knowledge and of your energy, my friend, I would not hesitate, under the pledge of secrecy, to tell you everything about it. But as it is I think that I must certainly prepare my own report of the matter before I expose myself to such formidable competition.'

Kennedy loved his subject with a love which was almost a mania – a love which held him true to it, amidst all the distractions which come to a wealthy and dissipated young man. He had ambition, but his ambition was secondary to his mere abstract joy and interest in everything which concerned the old life and history of the city. He yearned to see this new underworld which his companion had discovered.

'Look here, Burger,' said he, earnestly, 'I assure you that you can trust me most implicitly in the matter. Nothing would induce me to put pen to paper about anything which I see until I have your express permission. I quite understand your feeling and I think it is most natural, but you have really nothing whatever to fear from me. On the other hand, if you don't tell me I shall make a systematic search, and I shall most certainly discover it. In that case, of course, I should make what use I liked of it, since I should be under no obligation to you.'

Burger smiled thoughtfully over his cigar.

'I have noticed, friend Kennedy,' said he, 'that when I want information over any point you are not always so ready to supply it.'

'When did you ever ask me anything that I did not tell you? You remember, for example, my giving you the material for your paper about the temple of the Vestals.'

'Ah, well, that was not a matter of much importance. If I were to question you upon some intimate thing would you give me an answer, I wonder! This new catacomb is a very intimate thing to me, and I should certainly expect some sign of confidence in return.'

'What you are driving at I cannot imagine,' said the Englishman, 'but if you mean that you will answer my question about the catacomb if I answer any question which you may put to me I can assure you that I will certainly do so.'

'Well, then,' said Burger, leaning luxuriously back in his settee, and puffing a blue tree of cigar-smoke into the air, 'tell me all about your relations with Miss Mary Saunderson.'

Kennedy sprang up in his chair and glared angrily at his impassive companion.

'What the devil do you mean?' he cried. 'What sort of a question is this? You may mean it as a joke, but you never made a worse one.'

'No, I don't mean it as a joke,' said Burger, simply. 'I am really rather interested in the details of the matter. I don't know much about the world and women and social life and that sort of thing, and such an incident has the fascination of the unknown for me. I know you, and I knew her by sight – I had even spoken to her once or twice. I should very much like to hear from your own lips exactly what it was which occurred between you.'

'I won't tell you a word.'

'That's all right. It was only my whim to see if you would give up a secret as easily as you expected me to give up my secret of the new catacomb. You wouldn't, and I didn't expect you to. But why should you expect otherwise of me?

There's Saint John's clock striking ten. It is quite time that I was going home.'

'No; wait a bit, Burger,' said Kennedy; 'this is really a ridiculous caprice of yours to wish to know about an old love-affair which has burned out months ago. You know we look upon a man who kisses and tells as the greatest coward and villain possible.'

'Certainly,' said the German, gathering up his basket of curiosities, 'when he tells anything about a girl which is previously unknown he must be so. But in this case, as you must be aware, it was a public matter which was the common talk of Rome, so that you are not really doing Miss Mary Saunderson any injury by discussing her case with me. But still, I respect your scruples, and so good night!'

'Wait a bit, Burger,' said Kennedy, laying his hand upon the other's arm; 'I am very keen upon this catacomb business, and I can't let it drop quite so easily. Would you mind asking me something else in return – something not quite so eccentric this time?'

'No, no; you have refused, and there is an end of it,' said Burger, with his basket on his arm. 'No doubt you are quite right not to answer, and no doubt I am quite right also – and so again, my dear Kennedy, good night!'

The Englishman watched Burger cross the room, and he had his hand on the handle of the door before his host sprang up with the air of a man who is making the best of that which cannot be helped.

'Hold on, old fellow,' said he; 'I think you are behaving in a most ridiculous fashion; but still, if this is your condition, I suppose that I must submit to it. I hate saying anything about a girl, but, as you say, it is all over Rome, and I don't suppose I can tell you anything which you do not know already. What was it you wanted to know?'

The German came back to the stove, and, laying down his basket, he sank into his chair once more.

'May I have another cigar?' said he. 'Thank you very much! I never smoke when I work, but I enjoy a chat much more when I am under the influence of tobacco. Now, as regards this young lady, with whom you had this little adventure. What in the world has become of her?'

'She is at home with her own people.'

'Oh, really – in England?'

'Yes.'

'What part of England – London?'

'No, Twickenham.'

'You must excuse my curiosity, my dear Kennedy, and you must put it down to my ignorance of the world. No doubt it is quite a simple thing to persuade a young lady to go off with you for three weeks or so, and then to hand her over to her own family at – what did you call the place?'

'Twickenham.'

'Quite so – at Twickenham. But it is something so entirely outside my own experience that I cannot even imagine how you set about it. For example, if you had loved this girl your love could hardly disappear in three weeks, so I presume that you could not have loved her at all. But if you did not love her why should you make this great scandal which has damaged you and ruined her?'

Kennedy looked moodily into the red eye of the stove.

'That's a logical way of looking at it, certainly,' said he.

'Love is a big word, and it represents a good many different shades of feeling. I liked her, and – well, you say you've seen her – you know how charming she could look. But still I am willing to admit, looking back, that I could never have really loved her.'

'Then, my dear Kennedy, why did you do it?'

'The adventure of the thing had a great deal to do with it.'

'What! You are so fond of adventures!'

'Where would the variety of life be without them? It was for an adventure that I first began to pay my attentions to her. I've chased a good deal of game in my time, but there's no chase like that of a pretty woman. There was the piquant difficulty of it also, for, as she was the companion of Lady Emily Rood, it was almost impossible to see her alone. On the top of all the other obstacles which attracted me, I learned from her own lips very early in the proceedings that she was engaged.'

'Mein Gott! To whom?'

'She mentioned no names.'

'I do not think that anyone knows that. So that made the adventure more alluring, did it?'

'Well, it did certainly give a spice to it. Don't you think so?'

'I tell you that I am very ignorant about these things.'

'My dear fellow, you can remember that the apple you stole from your neighbour's tree was always sweeter than that which fell from your own. And then I found that she cared for me.'

'What – at once?'

'Oh, no, it took about three months of sapping and mining.

But at last I won her over. She understood that my judicial separation from my wife made it impossible for me to do the right thing by her – but she came all the same, and we had a delightful time, as long as it lasted.'

'But how about the other man?'

Kennedy shrugged his shoulders.

'I suppose it is the survival of the fittest,' said he. 'If he had been the better man she would not have deserted him. Let's drop the subject, for I have had enough of it!'

'Only one other thing. How did you get rid of her in three weeks?'

'Well, we had both cooled down a bit, you understand. She absolutely refused, under any circumstances, to come back to face the people she had known in Rome. Now, of course, Rome is necessary to me, and I was already pining to be back at my work – so there was one obvious cause of separation. Then again, her old father turned up at the hotel in London, and there was a scene, and the whole thing became so unpleasant that really – though I missed her dreadfully at first – I was very glad to slip out of it. Now, I rely upon you not to repeat anything of what I have said.'

'My dear Kennedy, I should not dream of repeating it. But all that you say interests me very much, for it gives me an insight into your way of looking at things, which is entirely different from mine, for I have seen so little of life. And now you want to know about my new catacomb. There's no use my trying to describe it, for you would never find it by that. There is only one thing, and that is for me to take you there.'

'That would be splendid.'

'When would you like to come?'

'The sooner the better. I am all impatience to see it.'

'Well, it is a beautiful night – though a trifle cold. Suppose we start in an hour. We must be very careful to keep the matter to ourselves. If anyone saw us hunting in couples they would suspect that there was something going on.'

'We can't be too cautious,' said Kennedy. 'Is it far?'

'Some miles.'

'Not too far to walk?'

'Oh, no, we could walk there easily'

'We had better do so, then. A cabman's suspicions would be aroused if he dropped us both at some lonely spot in the dead of the night.'

'Quite so. I think it would be best for us to meet at the Gate of the Appian Way at midnight. I must go back to my lodgings for the matches and candles and things.'

'All right, Burger! I think it is very kind of you to let me into this secret, and I promise you that I will write nothing about it until you have published your report. Good-bye for the present! You will find me at the Gate at twelve.'

The cold, clear air was filled with the musical chimes from that city of clocks as Burger, wrapped in an Italian overcoat, with a lantern hanging from his hand, walked up to the rendezvous. Kennedy stepped out of the shadow to meet him.

'You are ardent in work as well as in love!' said the German, laughing.

'Yes; I have been waiting here for nearly half an hour.'

'I hope you left no clue as to where we were going.'

'Not such a fool! By Jove, I am chilled to the bone! Come on, Burger, let us warm ourselves by a spurt of hard walking.'

Their footsteps sounded loud and crisp upon the rough

stone paving of the disappointing road which is all that is left of the most famous highway of the world. A peasant or two going home from the wine-shop, and a few carts of country produce coming up to Rome, were the only things which they met. They swung along, with the huge tombs looming up through the darkness upon each side of them, until they had come as far as the Catacombs of St Calixtus, and saw against a rising moon the great circular bastion of Cecilia Metella in front of them. Then Burger stopped with his hand to his side.

'Your legs are longer than mine, and you are more accustomed to walking,' said he, laughing. 'I think that the place where we turn off is somewhere here. Yes, this is it, round the corner of the trattoria. Now, it is a very narrow path, so perhaps I had better go in front and you can follow.'

He had lit his lantern, and by its light they were enabled to follow a narrow and devious track which wound across the marshes of the Campagna. The great Aqueduct of old Rome lay like a monstrous caterpillar across the moonlit landscape, and their road led them under one of its huge arches, and past the circle of crumbling bricks which marks the old arena. At last Burger stopped at a solitary wooden cow-house, and he drew a key from his pocket.

'Surely your catacomb is not inside a house!' cried Kennedy.

'The entrance to it is. That is just the safeguard which we have against anyone else discovering it.'

'Does the proprietor know of it?'

'Not he. He had found one or two objects which made me almost certain that his house was built on the entrance to such a place. So I rented it from him, and did my excavations for myself. Come in, and shut the door behind you.'

It was a long, empty building, with the mangers of the cows along one wall. Burger put his lantern down on the ground, and shaded its light in all directions save one by draping his overcoat round it.

'It might excite remark if anyone saw a light in this lonely place,' said he. 'Just help me to move this boarding.'

The flooring was loose in the corner, and plank by plank the two savants raised it and leaned it against the wall. Below there was a square aperture and a stair of old stone steps which led away down into the bowels of the earth.

'Be careful!' cried Burger, as Kennedy, in his impatience, hurried down them. 'It is a perfect rabbits' warren below, and if you were once to lose your way there the chances would be a hundred to one against your ever coming out again. Wait until I bring the light.'

'How do you find your own way if it is so complicated?'

'I had some very narrow escapes at first, but I have gradually learned to go about. There is a certain system to it, but it is one which a lost man, if he were in the dark, could not possibly find out. Even now I always spin out a ball of string behind me when I am going far into the catacomb. You can see for yourself that it is difficult, but every one of these passages divides and subdivides a dozen times before you go a hundred yards.'

They had descended some twenty feet from the level of the byre, and they were standing now in a square chamber cut out of the soft tufa. The lantern cast a flickering light, bright below and dim above, over the cracked brown walls.

In every direction were the black openings of passages which radiated from this common centre.

'I want you to follow me closely, my friend,' said Burger. 'Do not loiter to look at anything upon the way, for the place to which I will take you contains all that you can see, and more. It will save time for us to go there direct.'

He led the way down one of the corridors, and the Englishman followed closely at his heels. Every now and then the passage bifurcated, but Burger was evidently following some secret marks of his own, for he neither stopped nor hesitated. Everywhere along the walls, packed like the berths upon an emigrant ship, lay the Christians of old Rome. The yellow light flickered over the shrivelled features of the mummies, and gleamed upon rounded skulls and long, white armbones crossed over fleshless chests. And everywhere as he passed Kennedy looked with wistful eyes upon inscriptions, funeral vessels, pictures, vestments, utensils, all lying as pious hands had placed them so many centuries ago. It was apparent to him, even in those hurried, passing glances, that this was the earliest and finest of the catacombs, containing such a storehouse of Roman remains as had never before come at one time under the observation of the student.

'What would happen if the light went out?' he asked, as they hurried onwards.

'I have a spare candle and a box of matches in my pocket. By the way, Kennedy, have you any matches?'

'No; you had better give me some.'

'Oh, that is all right. There is no chance of our separating.'

'How far are we going? It seems to me that we have walked at least a quarter of a mile.'

'More than that, I think. There is really no limit to the tombs – at least, I have never been able to find any. This is a very difficult place, so I think that I will use our ball of string.'

He fastened one end of it to a projecting stone and he carried the coil in the breast of his coat, paying it out as he advanced. Kennedy saw that it was no unnecessary precaution, for the passages had become more complex and tortuous than ever, with a perfect network of intersecting corridors. But these all ended in one large circular hall with a square pedestal of tufa topped with a slab of marble at one end of it.

'By Jove!' cried Kennedy in an ecstasy, as Burger swung his lantern over the marble. 'It is a Christian altar – probably the first one in existence. Here is the little consecration cross cut upon the corner of it. No doubt this circular space was used as a church.'

'Precisely,' said Burger. 'If I had more time I should like to show you all the bodies which are buried in these niches upon the walls, for they are the early popes and bishops of the Church, with their mitres, their croziers, and full canonicals. Go over to that one and look at it!'

Kennedy went across, and stared at the ghastly head which lay loosely on the shredded and mouldering mitre.

'This is most interesting,' said he, and his voice seemed to boom against the concave vault. 'As far as my experience goes, it is unique. Bring the lantern over, Burger, for I want to see them all.'

But the German had strolled away, and was standing in the middle of a yellow circle of light at the other side of the hall.

'Do you know how many wrong turnings there are between this and the stairs?' he asked. 'There are over two thousand. No doubt it was one of the means of protection which the Christians adopted. The odds are two thousand to one against a man getting out, even if he had a light; but if he were in the dark it would, of course, be far more difficult.'

'So I should think.'

'And the darkness is something dreadful. I tried it once for an experiment. Let us try it again!' He stooped to the lantern, and in an instant it was as if an invisible hand was squeezed tightly over each of Kennedy's eyes. Never had he known what such darkness was. It seemed to press upon him and to smother him. It was a solid obstacle against which the body shrank from advancing. He put his hands out to push it back from him.

'That will do, Burger,' said he, 'let's have the light again.'

But his companion began to laugh, and in that circular room the sound seemed to come from every side at once.

'You seem uneasy, friend Kennedy,' said he.

'Go on, man, light the candle!' said Kennedy impatiently.

'It's very strange, Kennedy, but I could not in the least tell by the sound in which direction you stand. Could you tell where I am?'

'No; you seem to be on every side of me.'

'If it were not for this string which I hold in my hand I should not have a notion which way to go.'

'I dare say not. Strike a light, man, and have an end of this nonsense.'

'Well, Kennedy, there are two things which I understand that you are very fond of. The one is an adventure, and the other is an obstacle to surmount. The adventure must be the finding of your way out of this catacomb. The obstacle will be the darkness and the two thousand wrong turns which make the way a little difficult to find. But you need not hurry, for you have plenty of time, and when you halt for a rest now and then, I should like you just to think of Miss Mary Saunderson, and whether you treated her quite fairly.'

'You devil, what do you mean?' roared Kennedy. He was running about in little circles and clasping at the solid blackness with both hands.

'Good-bye,' said the mocking voice, and it was already at some distance. 'I really do not think, Kennedy, even by your own showing that you did the right thing by that girl. There was only one little thing which you appeared not to know, and I can supply it. Miss Saunderson was engaged to a poor ungainly devil of a student, and his name was Julius Burger.'

There was a rustle somewhere, the vague sound of a foot striking a stone, and then there fell silence upon that old Christian church – a stagnant, heavy silence which closed round Kennedy and shut him in like water round a drowning man.

Some two months afterwards the following paragraph made the round of the European Press:

One of the most interesting discoveries of recent years is that of the new catacomb in Rome, which lies some distance to the east of the well-known vaults of St Calixtus. The finding of this important burial-place, which is exceeding rich in most interesting early Christian remains, is due to the energy and sagacity of Dr Julius Burger, the young

German specialist, who is rapidly taking the first place as an authority upon ancient Rome. Although the first to publish his discovery, it appears that a less fortunate adventurer had anticipated Dr Burger. Some months ago Mr Kennedy, the well-known English student, disappeared suddenly from his rooms in the Corso, and it was conjectured that his association with a recent scandal had driven him to leave Rome. It appears now that he had in reality fallen a victim to that fervid love of archaeology which had raised him to a distinguished place among living scholars. His body was discovered in the heart of the new catacomb, and it was evident from the condition of his feet and boots that he had tramped for days through the tortuous corridors which make these subterranean tombs so dangerous to explorers. The deceased gentleman had, with inexplicable rashness, made his way into this labyrinth without, as far as can be discovered, taking with him either candles or matches, so that his sad fate was the natural result of his own temerity. What makes the matter more painful is that Dr Julius Burger was an intimate friend of the deceased. His joy at the extraordinary find which he has been so fortunate as to make has been greatly marred by the terrible fate of his comrade and fellow-worker.

The Motive

Ronald Knox

'A certain amount of dust is good for a juryman's eyes. It prevents him going to sleep.'

Sir Leonard Huntercombe is probably responsible for more scoundrels being at large than any other man in England. His references to the feelings of his client, to the long ordeal which a criminal prosecution involves, to the fallibility of witnesses, to those British liberties which we all enjoy only on the condition that everybody must be given the benefit of the doubt unless he is found with his hand in the till, are a subject of legitimate tedium and irreverent amusement to the reporters, who have heard it all before. But it still goes down with the jury, fresh to their job; and, after all, that is more important. It does not often happen to such a man that he is drawn into the old, old argument, whether a defending counsel is justified in pressing his defence when he privately knows his client to be guilty. And, of all places, you might have expected him to be free from such annoyances in the Senior Common Room of Simon Magus – the smoking-room, to be more accurate. Dons hate a scene, and prefer to talk trivialities after dinner. It is hardly even good form, nowadays, to talk a man's own shop to him. In these days of specialisation we are all bored with each other's technicalities, and a tacit convention has grown up that we should stick to the weather and the Boat Race. Sir Leonard was justified, then, if his eye resembled that of a codfish rather more than usual.

But, as bad luck would have it, Penkridge was dining as somebody else's guest – Penkridge, the dramatic critic, to whom all the world is a stage, and everything, consequently, a fit subject for dramatic criticism. It takes less than the Simon Magus port (though that is a powerful affair) to make such a man as Penkridge boorishly argumentative. He had trailed his coat deliberately, with a forthcoming article in view, and had contrived to put Sir Leonard on his own defence almost before he knew it. I need hardly say that he was adopting the most Puritan view of his subject. 'You wouldn't let me quote you as saying that?' he asked with a smirk; and Sir Leonard was forced to claim the privileges of a private discussion. What are common rooms for, if we are not to speak our minds in them?

McBride, the philosopher, was the host of the great man; and he felt bound to interfere, partly from a sense of hospitality, and partly because he always likes to be desperately just. (Nobody, it has been said, has seen more points of view than McBride, or adopted less.) 'I was just thinking,' he said, 'that perhaps you could put up an apology for Sir Leonard's point of view if you claim that Law should be regarded as one of the sciences. You see it's notorious, isn't it – I think even Cowan here will agree with me – that science owes some of its greatest developments to the influence of theories which have proved quite false, but were suggestive nevertheless, and put people on the track of the truth. Isn't it arguable, I mean, in the same way, that my friend here is justified in putting forward a hypothesis, which will help forward the cause of truth if only by eliminating error?'

Penkridge, who hates dons, was evidently preparing to say something unpleasant; but Sir Leonard forestalled him by disowning the proffered help. 'It's not a scientific mind you need in the legal profession,' he insisted; 'it's a kind of artistic gift. You've got to be imaginative; to throw yourself in the business of picturing the story happening as you want it to have happened; with your client innocent, of course. Probably, if we knew, we should find that the truth in many cases is even stranger than all our imaginings. But imagination is what you must have – did I ever tell you the story of a client of mine, McBride, a man by the name of Westmacott?'

Several voices demanded that the story should be told; better to have Sir Leonard being prosy, than Penkridge being unmannerly in his cups. And Sir Leonard, looking from time to time at the glowing end of his cigar, as if to derive inspiration from it, went ahead with the story, his fine voice, the envy of a hundred rivals, distracting the attention of the company from hunting noises now audible in the Quad., and the distant echoes of the Salvation Army.

'I first came across Westmacott,' explained Sir Leonard, 'over a business that never came into court, though it precious nearly did. I was only called in on a minor point to give counsel's opinion. He was a man in late middle age, with an unhealthy look about him, as if you wouldn't give him a very long life, and a depressed, restless sort of manner, as if his mind was preoccupied with something else than what he was talking about at the moment. He had done well on the Stock Exchange, and had retired just lately, with a considerable income he hardly knew what to do with. At least, it was a surprise to his friends when he went to stay over Christmas at one of those filthy great luxury hotels in Cornwall. It was the kind of place that tried to make you believe you were on the Riviera, with any amount of central heating and artificial sunlight, and a covered-in bathing-pool where the water was kept at a temperature of eighty or so, night and day. Of course, he might have gone to Cornwall for his health; but one didn't see why he should have gone to a place like that, because he was well known to be old fashioned in his views, and conservative in his opinions, whereas the Hotel Resplendent was all full of modern people, a cosmopolitan and rather Bohemian crowd. Among the rest there was a well-known literary man; he's still alive, and you'd all know his name, so I'll call him just Smith.

'I'm speaking of some years ago, you'll understand. Nowadays, of course, it doesn't matter what anybody writes, or what sort of opinions he puts forward; it's all art. But at the time of which I'm speaking, there were still people going about who were capable of being shocked, and they were shocked by Smith. It wasn't so much his indecency, though every book he wrote looked as if it was meant to be seized by the police. He was really, if an old fogy like myself can be allowed to use such forgotten language, a bad influence on the young people; everybody admitted it, though already most people rather admired him for it. Westmacott had never met him before, and the other people in the hotel felt pretty certain that the two wouldn't hit it off. The curious thing is, they were wrong. Westmacott hadn't read any of Smith's stuff, it appeared; indeed, he read very little except detective stories, which he devoured at the rate of one a day. And — well, strange acquaintances do ripen, and ripen fast, in a god-forsaken place like the Hotel Resplendent.

'It was a bad season; money wasn't being thrown about that year as much as usual; and the management tried to make the best of the position by encouraging the guests to be a sort of family party, with any amount of "olde-worlde" festivities. Naturally, they concentrated on Christmas Day; crackers and Christmas presents, and a synthetic boar's head, and a Yule-log specially imported from Sweden; and a set of waits who'd been in training under an opera expert for months past. By half-past ten the company — between twenty and thirty of them, when you'd counted out the invalids who'd gone to bed early, and the idiots who'd gone out in cars for no reason whatever — found themselves set down by the master of the revels to play "blind man's buff". This didn't go too well, especially as the great hall, in which they played it, was heated like a crematorium. It was Westmacott, people remembered afterwards, who made the suggestion you would have expected to come from anybody but West-macott — that they should all go and play "blind man's buff" in the swimming-bath.

'Well, they got some kick out of it after that. Westmacott

didn't go in himself, but he hung about on the edge; as a matter of fact, it was only pretty strong swimmers who did go in, because the bath was a matter of twelve feet deep at the shallowest part, and there was nothing but a handrail to lug yourself out by. Smith and Westmacott got into an argument; Westmacott saying he didn't believe you could know what direction you were swimming in when you were blindfolded, and Smith (who was an exceptionally good swimmer himself) maintaining that it was perfectly easy, unless you'd got a bad sense of direction anyhow. It was nearly midnight when the party went away, and it seems that Smith and Westmacott stayed behind to settle their differences with a practical try-out and a bet: Smith was to swim ten lengths in the bath each way, touching the ends every time, but never touching the sides. They were quite alone when Westmacott adjusted the handkerchief on his new friend's forehead, to make sure that everything was above board.

'Well, Smith did his ten lengths each way, and by his own account made a good thing of it. As he swam he didn't bother to touch the handrail, which was rather high out of the water; but when he'd finished he naturally felt for it, and it wasn't there. He tore the handkerchief off his eyes, which wasn't too easy, and found the whole place was in the dark. The rail wasn't within his reach anywhere, and he tumbled to what must have happened. Somehow a goodish lot of water must have been let out of the bath while he wasn't looking; and there was nothing to do but go on swimming about until somebody came to put things right for him; or, alternatively, until the level of the water fell so much that he was able to stand on the bottom.

'Other things began to occur to him before long. For one thing, he knew, more or less, where it was that the water escaped when the bath was changed, and he knew that there was a considerable undertow when it happened. He found there was no undertow now, which meant that the water wasn't escaping any longer, and there was no chance of finding that he'd got into his depth. Also, he remembered that the swimming-bath was a long way from anywhere, and it wasn't very likely that he would be heard if he shouted. Also, he couldn't quite see how the water could have started emptying itself and then stopped, unless somebody was controlling it, or why anybody should be controlling it in that odd way for any legitimate purpose.

And he found himself beginning to suspect that his new friend Westmacott had, for some unaccountable reason, left him deliberately there to drown.

'Well, they say the devil looks after his own, and it so happened that the night watchman, whom they kept at the Hotel Resplendent (chiefly to keep out of the way when he wasn't wanted), had spotted that the water was running away, and mentioned it to somebody; a search was made, and Smith was pulled out of the water with a rope, none too soon for his peace of mind. Smith was positive, of course, that he had been the victim of a particularly cunning murderous attack. I say particularly cunning, because, once he had drowned, it would have been easy for Westmacott (he assumed Westmacott was the villain) to have let the water into the bath again; and all the world would have been left supposing that Smith had committed suicide – how else could a strong swimmer have drowned with a handrail in his reach all the time? It looked as if it was going to be a very nasty business, and what didn't make it any better was Westmacott's own explanation, made privately to his lawyers, that the whole thing was a joke, and he had been meaning to rescue Smith later on. Nothing, it was explained to him, is more difficult to predict than a jury's sense of humour. Enormous efforts were made to hush the thing up, chiefly by the hotel people, who thought it meant the end of their business if they were involved in a scandal; I'm not sure they were right there, but, as I say, this happened some years ago. The difficulty of Smith's case was that there was no proving it was Westmacott who had tampered with the water apparatus (as a matter of fact, anybody could have done it), and it was that hitch that induced the police to let it go; and Smith to be content with a handsome compensation. His publishers were furious; they had got wind of it somehow, and were hoping to sell a mammoth edition of his next book on the strength of his news-value.

'Well, it was touch and go, and there was nothing I expected less than to find Westmacott, to all appearances a dull and unadventurous man, figuring in my line of business again. Though, as a matter of fact, the police had found out things about him which would have altered my opinion if I'd known about them. His man, fortunately for the police, had done time at an earlier stage in his career, and was all too ready to give them information. He assured them that a great change had come over his master within the last week or so before he went to the Resplendent; he had come home one morning looking like a man bowed down by some hideous secret anxiety, though up to then he had been in normally good spirits. He cursed the servants freely, he would start at shadows. He bought a revolver, which the police found in his rooms (he was a bachelor, I forgot to say); and although this only looked like self-defence, it was a more peculiar circumstance that, about the same time, he got hold of a drug (I forget the name of it now) which is deadly poison, and I'm not sure that he hadn't forged a doctor's certificate to get it. It was a marvel, I told him later, that the law didn't prosecute; what had saved him, I fancy, was that the police had been made to look fools in one or two recent trials ... Yes, you're right; I had a hand in it.

'It was less than a week after the trouble had died down that a new character came on the scene: a character nobody liked, who had seen him. He was a seedy-looking fellow calling himself Robinson, who seemed very anxious to have an interview with Westmacott, for he made a great fuss with the servants when he called three times and found he was always out. It was the opinion of the servants that Robinson went about in disguise for no good end, but servants will always say that of anybody who wears dark spectacles. When the two did first meet, the servants weren't prepared to say, because Westmacott lived on one floor, and often let in his visitors himself. Anyhow, for a fortnight or so he was a familiar in the house, being seen several times coming in and out. The servants got to know his address, too, in a rather poky part of West Kensington: Westmacott wrote to him more than once. That came in useful later on.

'Westmacott had the habit of going to stay with friends near Aberdeen about the New Year. This time, he went a little later than usual; and it was a considerable surprise to his man when he was given the order to reserve two first-class sleepers on the night train from King's Cross, one in the name of Westmacott, and another in the name of Robinson. It didn't look too good; you couldn't by any stretch of the imagination suppose that Robinson belonged to the same world as Westmacott and his friends. In fact, if he hadn't been professionally shy of them, I think the man would have gone to the police about it; it looked so much as if Robinson had got a hold of some kind over Westmacott, and was following him about for fear of losing his tracks. Anyhow, nothing was done about it. Westmacott was a man who fussed about trains, and he was at the station, it seems, a full three-quarters of an hour before the train started; he was worried, apparently, about Robinson – asked the attendant once or twice whether he had shown up yet, and stood looking up and down the platform. As he did this, a telegram was brought to him which seemed to set his mind at rest; he shut himself up in his sleeper, and took no further notice, as far as could be ascertained. Robinson turned up with only two or three minutes to spare, and was bundled hurriedly into the sleeper next door. Whether the two held any conversation was not known; the two sleepers communicated with one another in the ordinary way, and it was only a matter of slipping a bolt for either to enter the other's compartment.

'Robinson, it appeared, was not travelling all the way to Aberdeen; he was to get off at Dundee. The man was to come and call him about three-quarters of an hour before the train got in there. As a matter of fact, he cannot have slept too well, or possibly the lights and the shouting at Edinburgh woke him; at any rate, he went along the corridor just about when they were passing Dalmeny, and spoke to the attendant, who asked whether the order to call him still stood. He said yes, he expected to drop off again for a bit, and he was a heavy sleeper. Indeed, when the attendant knocked at his door, there seemed to be no waking him, and it was locked. With many apologies, the man knocked up Westmacott, and asked his leave to try the communicating door between the two compartments. This, it proved, was locked on Westmacott's side, but not on Robinson's. The attendant went in, and found the carriage quite empty. The bed had been slept in; that is, somebody had lain down on it, there was no mistaking the fact. Robinson's luggage was still there; his watch was hanging by the bunk; a novel he had been reading lay on the floor close by; his boots were there, and his day clothes, not his pyjamas. But Robinson was nowhere to be found.

'Well, there was all sorts of fuss and bother, as you can imagine. Westmacott, who seemed quite dazed by the news and unable to give any account of it, naturally got out at Dundee and put himself at the disposal of the police authorities. They did not like the look of the thing from the start. They had rung up Scotland Yard, and through some unwonted piece of efficiency had got on to the story of Smith and his experiences in the bath at the Resplendent. Exhaustive inquiries brought no news of Robinson being seen anywhere on the line; and there had been no stop, no slowdown, even, between the time when the attendant saw him in the corridor and the time when his bed was found empty. The train, naturally, had been searched, but without result.'

'But they must have found his body,' someone suggested.

'No remains were found; but you have to consider the lie

of the journey. Between Dalmeny and Thornoton Junction, near which the attendant tried to wake Robinson, the train has to pass over the Forth Bridge. The one interval of time, therefore, during which it was impossible to account for Robinson's movements was an interval of time during which a body might, conceivably, have been got rid of without leaving any trace. To disappear, it would have to be weighted, no doubt. But the awkward fact emerged that Westmacott brought a very heavy bag with him into the train (the porter gave evidence of this), and it was completely empty when examined. This was one of the things that made the prosecution feel really hopeful about their case. There seemed no other way of accounting for the odd circumstance.

'As I say, I thought Westmacott had been lucky to get off so lightly in the Resplendent affair. I didn't at all like the look of his case when I was asked to plead for him. When I went to see him I found him all broken up and in tears. He told me a long story in which he confessed to the murder of Robinson. Robinson – it was the old story – had been blackmailing him; he had evidence that it was Westmacott who attempted the murder of Smith in Cornwall. I gathered that there were other secrets behind it all which Westmacott was not anxious to go into, but it was the fear of exposure over the Smith case that made him reluctant to bring in the police against the blackmailer. Robinson had insisted on following him when he went north, afraid that he was trying to escape to the Continent by way of Leith or Aberdeen. The knowledge that he was being shadowed like this was too much for him, and he determined to get rid of his persecutor. Arranging for him to travel in the next carriage, he waited till the train was past Dalmeny, then found his man asleep, and laid him out with a piece of lead, tied that and other weights onto him as he lay there, and threw him out of the window just as the train was crossing the Forth Bridge. His error had been that he neglected to unlock the door from Robinson's compartment into the corridor. If that had been left open it would have been hard to prove that Robinson had ever gone back there – though it was difficult, in any case, to account for his movements.

'Ordinarily, when a man charged with murder tells you he is guilty you can form a pretty good guess between the two obvious alternatives – either he is telling the truth or he ought to be in an asylum. Occasionally there is a third possibility, for which the present circumstances did not seem to leave any room: he may be inculpating himself to save somebody else. I tell you, I didn't know what to make of it. The whole story seemed wrong; Westmacott was not a strong man, and what would he have done if his man had not been asleep? The chances are enormously against any man sleeping soundly on a train. Why, too, was Westmacott so keen to throw the body overboard at a place where it would remain undiscovered, when the circumstances were bound, in any case, to raise the suspicion of murder against him? If the prosecution depended on such an improbable story as that, I felt I could make mincemeat of it.

'Now, what was I to do? I felt certain the man was not mad, and I have seen many lunatics in my time. I did not, could not, believe he was really guilty. I put it to you whether, with those convictions in my mind, I was not really offering to serve the cause of truth when I urged him (as of course I did) to plead "Not guilty". Or, at least, as McBride would say, I was proposing to eliminate the chances of error.

'He would have none of it – then. It was only a day or two later that I had an impassioned appeal to go and see him again. I found his mind entirely altered. He still stuck to his story that Robinson had been blackmailing him, but he professed to know nothing whatever about the disappearance: he thought Robinson must have either committed suicide or else staged a very clever disappearance with the sole intention of bringing him, Westmacott, to the dock. He implored me to save him from the gallows. This was too much for me; I couldn't undertake to plead for a man who didn't know from one day to the next whether he was guilty or not guilty, and gave such very lame explanations of his movements and his motives in either case. At last, when I had been at him some time, he told me a third story, which was quite different, and, as I believe, true. I shan't tell you what it was just yet. As I say, I thought, and think, it was true. But it was obvious to me from the first that it was a story you could not possibly serve up to a jury.

'There was another odd thing, which was that now, for reasons you will understand later, I did not know whether I wanted my man hanged or not. I don't know how some of you severe moralists would have formed your consciences in a situation like that. I thanked God I could fall back on a legal tradition, and I resolved that I would defend Westmacott, devoting myself single-heartedly to pointing out the weaknesses in the story, whatever it was, the prosecution would bring against him. And, gentlemen, I succeeded. I don't think I have ever had a tougher fight; there was any amount of prejudice against him among the public at large, and the jury, as usual, reflected it. But there was the solid fact that no body had been found; the open possibility that Robinson had made away with himself, or slipped off somehow when the train stopped. And, of course, the difficulty of throwing a body clear of the bridge. There was a mass of circumstantial evidence, but not a line of direct proof. And the jury sometimes, though not by any means always, will give its verdict according to the form book. Westmacott was acquitted, and the warder who went up to congratulate him found him in floods of tears. Of course, you see what had happened.'

McBride, who had been sitting with his head buried in his hands, lifted it slowly. 'I expect I'm being a fool,' he said, 'but I don't believe there was any such person as Robinson. He was just Westmacott, wasn't he?'

'That's a theory to go on, at all events,' admitted Sir Leonard, accepting the whisky-and-soda with which the suggestion was accompanied. 'Let's hear your reasons for thinking that, and I'll put the difficulties.'

'Well, as you've told the story, nobody ever saw the two men together. When Robinson was seen going out of the house, it was supposed to be Westmacott who had let him in. At the station, there was nothing to prevent Westmacott getting out of his sleeper during that last quarter of an hour, going off somewhere, and putting on the Robinson disguise, picking up fresh luggage at the cloakroom, and so making his second appearance. He made sure that the attendant should see him at Dalmeny, because he wanted everybody to think that Robinson had been thrown overboard exactly at the Forth Bridge. There was no point in making the body disappear when all the circumstances would, in any case, point to murder – unless there was no body to disappear.'

'Good for you, McBride; I like to hear a man put a case well. And now let me point out the difficulties. You've got to suppose that a man who has already laboured under an awkward imputation of intended murder deliberately projects an *alter ego* – a sort of Mr Hyde – for no better purpose than to get rid of his imaginary carcass, thereby letting himself in for a second dose of suspicion. That, having done so, he first of all pretends to his counsel that he is really a murderer, and then he withdraws it all and decides to plead "Not guilty". Can you give a coherent account of all that?'

'The man was barmy,' suggested Penkridge.

'Who isn't, up to a point? But there was certainly method in poor Westmacott's madness. Shall I tell you the story he told me?'

'We'll buy it!' agreed Penkridge.

'I wonder if you could have guessed it? If so, your guesswork would have had to start from the moment at which, if you remember, Westmacott suddenly came home one day a changed man, with the shadow of something over his life. You see, he had been feeling ill for some time. He had made an appointment with a specialist, and that specialist told him the worst he had been afraid of hearing. Not only were his days numbered, but he must look forward to months of increasing pain, during which, very probably, his reason would be affected. That is the whole story; the rest just flows from it.

'Westmacott hated pain, perhaps more than most of us. He was not capable of facing great endurance, whether in action or in suffering. It didn't take him long to realise that there was only one thing for him to do – to cut his life short by suicide. He went out and bought a revolver with the necessary ammunition. He shut himself up with it, and found that his hand was that of a physical coward; it would not pull the trigger. He tried long-distance methods, bought some poison, and tried to dose himself with it. Even here he had no better success. He realised, with self-loathing, that he was a man who could not take his own life.

'It is open to you to say, if you like, that something went wrong with his brain after that, but if he had the makings of a lunatic, his was the logic of lunacy. If he could not kill himself, he must make somebody else do it for him. He had not the physique to embark on some arduous adventure: fighting, for example, or a difficult mountain climb. Bravoes cannot be hired nowadays. There was only one way of inducing somebody else to kill him, and that was to kill somebody else. He must get himself condemned to the gallows.

'Well, as you see, he went about that in a painstaking way. He deliberately went and stayed at that appalling hotel because he knew that he would meet there the sort of people he most disliked. He found himself in luck; Smith was there, and Smith was a man who, in his view, would be all the better for extermination. Circumstances favoured him, too, in showing him a way to achieve his end. With all that reading of detective stories, you see, he had become fantastically ingenious in his conceptions of crime. He laid a trap for his victim which would make it possible for him to effect the murder by merely turning a tap, and then turning it a second time. There would be no blood, no struggle, no circumstances of violence. The only thing he failed to observe – or was he, after all, half-hearted in his desire for the gallows? – was that his excessive ingenuity might have made it hard to secure a conviction against him.

'As it was, something worse happened. By mere accident, the crime of murder reduced itself to that of attempted murder, and penal servitude was no use to him. Rather sheepishly, he had to try and pass it off as a joke; all he had gained was the assurance that when he was next accused of murder, people would be apt to believe it against him. He did not attempt a second murder, which might go as wrong as the first one had gone wrong. He brought Mr Robinson into existence, and then hurried him out of existence in the way you have all heard; he had got what he wanted.

'And then, of course, the coward came out in him again, and the close prospect of the gallows frightened him more than the remote prospect of a painful death later on. He broke down, and told me the story as I have been telling it to you. And I saved him; but for the life of me I did not know whether I was doing him a benefit in trying to save him. I simply had to proceed by rule of thumb, and behave as a good advocate should.'

'What became of him?' asked McBride.

'Fate stepped in, if you like to call it that. As he left the court, rather dazed with all he had gone through, he stumbled at the edge of the pavement in a crowded street, and a lorry was on the top of him before, I think, he knew what was happening. No, I saw it, and I am certain he didn't throw himself off the pavement. I don't believe he could have, either.'

'There's just one comment your story suggests to me,' objected Penkridge, bitter to the last. 'I always thought a lawyer was not allowed to repeat the story told him in confidence by his client?'

'That is why I said that the great gift in the legal profession is imaginativeness. You see, I have been making it all up as I went along.'

Dog in the Night-Time

Edmund Crispin

Gervase Fen, Professor of English Language and Literature in the University of Oxford, found Ann Cargill waiting for him in his rooms in college when he returned there from dinner at the George on a certain bitter February evening.

She was a quiet, good-looking girl, the most pleasant, if not the brightest, of the few undergraduates to whom he gave private tuition.

'Nice to see you back,' he said. For he knew that Ann's father had recently died, and that she had been given leave of absence for the first few weeks of term in order to cope with the situation and its aftermath.

'It's not about work, I'm afraid,' she confessed. 'Not altogether, I mean. I – I was wondering if you could help me over something – something personal.'

'Surely your moral tutor—' Fen began, and then suddenly remembered who Ann's moral tutor was. 'No,' he said.

'No, of course not ... Wait while I get us some drinks, and then you can tell me all about it.'

'I'm probably being several sorts of a fool,' said Ann, as soon as they were settled with glasses in their hands. 'But here goes, anyway ... I don't know if you know anything about my family, but my mother died years ago. I'm an only child, and my father – well, the important thing about him, for the moment, is that he had a passion for jewels.

'Jewels weren't his business. They were his hobby. And two or three months ago he sank an enormous amount of money – about three-quarters of his capital, I should think – into buying a single diamond that he'd set his heart on, a huge thing, quite flawless.

'Well, now, at the beginning of this year Daddy shut up our house at Abingdon – I live on my own in the vacs, you see, in a flat in Town; he liked me to do that – and flew out to Australia on business. He didn't take the diamond with him. It was left in the house—'

Fen lifted his eyebrows.

'Ah, yes, but the point is, it was really quite as safe there as it would have been in the bank. At the time he started collecting jewels Daddy had his study made as near burglar-proof as money could buy; and there was only one set of keys to the door and the safe; and when he went to Australia he left those with Mr Spottiswoode, his solicitor.'

Ann took a deep breath. 'And then he – he was killed. In a street accident in Sydney ... I – I went down to Abingdon after the wire came, and wandered about there a bit. Remembering. That was when I saw Mr Spottiswoode, the solicitor, driving away from the house.

'I don't think he saw me. I called after him, but he didn't stop. And, of course, being Daddy's executor, he had a perfect right to be there. But I always hated Mr Spottiswoode …'

Ann wriggled in her chair. 'And I'm pretty sure,' she added, 'that he was a crook.'

After a brief pause: 'I've no proof of that,' she went on. 'And you don't have to believe it if you don't want to. I only mentioned it because it's one of the reasons why I've come to you. Mr Spottiswoode—'

'You say he "was" a crook.'

'Yes, that's the next thing. Mr Spottiswoode's dead, you see. He died three weeks ago, very soon after I saw him at Abingdon; quite suddenly of a heart attack. And at that stage he hadn't yet got what they call a grant of probate of Daddy's will.

'So that what's happened since, is that my Uncle Harry, who's now my legal guardian, has been made administrator of the estate on my behalf. In other words, Mr Spottiswoode *did* have the keys to Daddy's study and Uncle Harry has them *now*.'

'And is Uncle Harry a crook too?'

Ann wriggled still more. 'I know it must sound as if I've got some hellish great neurosis, persecution mania or something, but – well, yes, frankly I think he is. Only not the same kind as Mr Spottiswoode. Uncle Harry's the rather nice, inefficient, sentimental sort of crook who always gets caught sooner or later.'

'In which case we must hope that it's he who has stolen your father's diamond, and not Mr Spottiswoode,' said Fen briskly. 'I take it that theft is what you have in mind?'

'It's crazy I know, and we shall probably find the diamond in the safe where Daddy put it. But – look, Professor Fen: Uncle Harry's meeting me at the house tomorrow morning to unlock the study and – and go through its contents. He's been in America up to five days ago, so there hasn't been a chance before. If I could just have someone with me ...'

And Fen nodded. 'I'll come,' he said. For he had known Ann Cargill long enough to be aware that, however erratic her views on *Beowulf* or Dryden, she was nobody's fool.

Uncle Harry proved to be a big, florid, amiable man dressed in checks with a black arm-band. And like his niece, he appeared at the Abingdon house next morning with a companion.

'Humbleby!' said Fen, pleased; and: 'Well, well,' said Detective Inspector Humbleby of Scotland Yard as he shook Fen's hand: 'And what are you doing here?'

'Looking for a diamond,' said Fen. 'Miss Cargill is a pupil of mine ... Ann, meet the inspector.'

'We're all looking for a diamond,' said Uncle Harry. 'And from what the inspector told me yesterday, there's a damn good chance we shan't find one.'

'Twenty thousand pounds,' said Humbleby, 'is somewhere about what the average high-class fence would give for a diamond like your father's, Miss Cargill. And £20,000 is what Mr Spottiswoode's executors found hidden in his house after his death. Being honest men, they came and had a word with us about it at the Yard. We've been working on the case for a fortnight now, and we still don't know where that money came from. Nothing legitimate, you can be sure ...

'But there was never any secret about your father's buying that jewel; and his death was reported in the papers; and his name was on the list of Mr Spottiswoode's clients. So of course we started putting two and two together, and yesterday I had a word with your uncle about it, and he very kindly invited me down here, subject to your having no objection—'

'Of course not,' said Ann.

'So that now,' Humbleby concluded, 'we shall see what we shall see.'

A woman, Ann explained, had been coming in once or twice a week to keep the house dusted, but her ministrations had not, of course, included the study, which would undoubtedly be in a mess. And so it turned out.

When Uncle Harry had manipulated the elaborate locks, thrown the study door open and switched on the lights (for the room was in darkness, thanks to the solid steel shutters on the windows), they saw that dust – five weeks' dust – lay undisturbed on the furniture, the bare polished boards of the floor, everything.

Also it was cold in there: while Uncle Harry fumbled with the safe, Ann turned on the big electric fire and stood warming her hands at it. Presently, Fen, who had been peering at the marks left by their feet on the dusty floor, lifted his head and sniffed.

'Is there something burning?' he asked suspiciously.

They all sniffed. 'I can't smell anything,' said Ann. 'Nor me,' said Humbleby. 'Nor me,' said Uncle Harry, pausing in his labour: and added ruefully, 'But then, it's years since I was able to smell anything.'

Fen shrugged. 'My mistake,' he said. Though as a matter of fact it had not been a mistake, since he himself had not been able to smell anything burning, either. His eye caught Humbleby's. 'Dog,' he confided solemnly, 'in the night-time.'

Humbleby scowled. 'Dog in the—'

'Eureka!' said Uncle Harry inaccurately: actually, all he had contrived to do so far was to get the safe door open. But a moment later he emerged from it holding a handsome jewel-box. 'Would this be—'

'Yes, that's it,' said Ann. 'Open it, please.'

And Uncle Harry opened it. And it was empty.

'It couldn't,' Humbleby suggested, 'be somewhere else?'

'No.' Ann shook her head decisively. 'I was with my father just before he left, and that was where he put it.'

Uncle Harry grunted. 'Anyway, there's your explanation of Spottiswoode's £20,000.'

But Fen apparently did not agree. 'No,' he said. 'Insufflator.'

'Beg pardon?'

'Insufflator. For example, one of those rubber-bulb things barbers use for blowing powder onto your chin. And dust, as such, isn't really very hard to come by. It would take a little time, and a little care, but I'm willing to bet that given twenty-four hours you could re-dust the entire room.'

An ugly gleam had appeared in Uncle Harry's eye. 'Just what,' he enunciated slowly, 'are you suggesting?'

'I was suggesting a likely means for you to have used to cover up your traces after stealing the diamond. You stole it last night, I suppose, after Humbleby's account of Spottiswoode's hoard — which I should guess is probably blackmail money accumulated over a good many years – had suggested to you how you could disperse the blame. As to why Spottiswoode didn't forestall you – well, it may simply be that he didn't know of any means of disposing of such a distinctive stone.'

'The man's mad,' said Uncle Harry, with conviction. 'Now look, sir: granted I *could* have stolen the diamond and then covered my traces with all this – this insufflator rubbish, what the devil makes you think I actually *did*? Where's your evidence, man, your proof?'

'*Dog?*'

'Like this electric fire, here,' Fen explained. 'No smell of burning, you recall, when it was first switched on. But there *ought* to have been a smell of burning if the fire had been accumulating dust since (at the latest) Spottiswoode's death three weeks ago. Ask any housewife. Ergo, the fire had been very recently used ...

'And I'm afraid, Mr Cargill, that that means you.'

Credits